a convenient escape

A PRIDE AND PREJUDICE VARIATION

CECILIA NORMAN

Copyright © 2023 by Celia Norman

All rights reserved.

No part of this book may be reproduced in any form or by any electronic or mechanical means, including information storage and retrieval systems, without written permission from the author, except for the use of brief quotations in a book review.

ONE
elizabeth bennet

"DO you really think it is appropriate for me to attend this ball?"

I was nervous, and it was impossible to hide it.

"Nonsense," my aunt said with a smile. "Now, come out from behind that screen and let me look at you."

I took a deep breath and smoothed my hands over the smooth muslin of my borrowed gown. It was beautiful, I could not argue with that, but I rarely wore this color of lilac, and I was uncertain about the neckline... my father would certainly not have approved of it, but my mother would have been overjoyed to see me dressed in such a manner.

"The very best of London fashion," my aunt exclaimed. "You look so well in your day dresses, Lizzy, and I am certain that there is no need for you to be so shy now. Come along!"

My aunt clapped her hands and I had no choice but to step out from behind the privacy screen that had been set up in my bedchamber.

"The gown is lovely—" I began.

"Lovely!" Mrs. Gardiner cried. "Why, you will be the envy of all the young ladies at the ball tonight! I have never seen you wear lilac, Lizzy... you should do so more often. I shall write to your mother to tell her so."

My cheeks were already warm but as soon as I caught sight of myself in the vanity mirror, I wanted to dive back behind the screen and change back into my plain day dress that had been re-hemmed and mended far too many times.

"Come closer," my aunt exclaimed as she fussed with the dark aubergine ribbons at the shoulders of the gown. "I knew I was right to choose this gown. Miss Lily will be so pleased that you are able to wear it."

"You must send her my thanks," I said. "Shall I write to her?"

"You will be able to express your gratitude in person at the ball," my aunt said with a smile.

"It is only—"

"This is your first London ball," my aunt interrupted. "I know. But you must think of it precisely the same way you do a Meryton ball... except that there will be enough gentlemen in attendance to see that every young lady has a dancing partner."

"That will be different," I murmured.

"I have told your mother on many occasions that there will be no hope of finding you girls suitable husbands if you do not come to London..." My aunt stepped back and set her hands on her hips as she looked me up and down. "There," she said. "Perfection. I shall lend you some of my silver hairpins, and we shall go into Market Street to find more ribbon to match that beautiful aubergine. It will look so lovely in your hair. And perhaps some white flowers, too."

"If you think that would be best."

My aunt nodded. "I do, indeed. Look at yourself in the mirror, Lizzy. You must admit that you look very lovely."

I smiled at my aunt's enthusiasm. "I shall take your word

for it, aunt. You always know best when it comes to such things."

"It is a pity that Jane did not come to London with you," Mrs. Gardiner mused. "But perhaps it is best if you all come separately... I would not wish to overwhelm London with Bennet sisters on the lookout for husbands."

I couldn't help but laugh at my aunt's words. My sisters and I were certainly not on the prowl for husbands, but I suppose it was the expectation of young ladies of our station.

As my aunt continued to fuss with my hair and ribbons, my mind wandered to the prospect of finding a suitable husband. It was not that I was desperate for marriage, but I knew it was an inevitability. If anyone had asked, I would have told them that I would have been quite happy to be left to my own devices with my books... but that was not an answer that was expected of young ladies. Even ones who had lived their entire lives in the country away from the business and excitement of London and its society.

I had met and danced with my fair share of gentlemen in Meryton, but none had ever captured my heart or my interest. I could not imagine a life spent as the wife of any of the officers or gentlemen in Hertfordshire, which my mother was certain was my main failing.

Your standards are far too high for our station, my dear...

My aunt must have sensed my anxiety, for she squeezed my hand reassuringly. "You will do fine, my dear," she said. "Just remember to smile and be gracious, and the rest will fall into place."

I took a deep breath and smiled at my aunt. "I do not wish to disappoint you."

"And you never will," Mrs. Gardiner replied. "My dear, Lizzy. It is a ball, and there will be nothing out of the ordinary that will happen. You will see."

She released my hand and bustled about the room as I stepped back behind the screen to change out of the beautiful gown that Miss Lily Trainor had lent me.

"How well do you know Lady Blackridge?" I asked.

"Well enough to be invited to her spring ball every year," my aunt replied. I could hear the humor in her voice and knew that it was also a small admonition to stop worrying... I was terrible at that, and she knew it.

As I shrugged out of the gown and laid it over the back of a chair, my aunt hummed a merry little tune, and I tried to push aside my anxieties over the evening ahead.

"Get dressed, we still have time to walk to Market Street," my aunt said. "Unless you'd like me to send one of the kitchen girls? I'm sure they would be glad of the distraction from their day."

I pulled my plain ivory day dress over my head, secured the ribbons at my shoulders, and then smoothed down my hair as I stepped out from behind the screen. "Oh, no," I said. "I should be glad of some exercise and fresh air. We can leave whenever you like."

My aunt's smile was warm. "Then we shall leave at once."

* * *

HOURS LATER, dressed and ready for Lady Blackridge's ball, I was a bundle of nerves all over again. I kept catching glimpses of myself in the parlor windows and the glass in my aunt's china cabinet, and each time I had to stop and remind myself that it was actually me in the reflection.

The lilac gown and aubergine ribbons were stylish and striking, and I felt far too grand for my own good... Lydia would have laughed to see me so uncomfortable.

"You must not worry, Lizzy. You are a smart, beautiful

young lady with a good head on your shoulders. Any gentleman would be lucky to have you as his wife."

I knew that my aunt was trying her best to reassure me, and I tried to smile at her words. She had every hope that she would be the one to help me find a husband... if I could find a gentleman to marry, surely my other sisters would have a much easier time of it.

But deep down, I knew that finding a suitable husband was not going to be easy. I had my own set of standards and expectations... Standards that would not easily be met. It did not help matters that I refused to compromise those standards just so I could call myself a wife and escape Longbourn and perhaps even Hertfordshire...

That was not the life I wanted.

"The carriage will be arriving soon," my aunt said. "And you must stop pacing, you are making me nervous."

I sank down into a chair and clasped my gloved hands in my lap. "I do apologize," I murmured. "It is only—"

"Is there anything I can say that will calm your nerves?" my aunt asked kindly.

My fingers twisted together as I met my aunt's steady gaze. "What— What might I expect to happen tonight?"

My aunt's smile was reassuring. "Well, as I said it is much like any ball that you have attended in Meryton, I should think. There will be drinks, dancing, wonderful musicians... cards if you do not wish to dance. Although I daresay you are a much more delightful dancer than you are a card player..."

"Very amusing," I muttered as my aunt laughed. "But what if I do not know any of the dances?" I asked. It was a fear that had plagued me since my aunt had told me about the ball.

"I would not be worried at all," she said. "If you explain to your partner that you are unfamiliar with the dance I am certain that you will find all the assistance that you require. And Miss Lily Trainor has promised to look out for you."

Her words did little to assuage my nerves, but I nodded all the same. "Thank you, aunt. And what of the gentlemen?" I asked. "What might I expect from them?"

My aunt paused, thoughtful. "Well, you should expect them to be polite, charming, and eager to dance with you. It is a ball, after all, and you are a new face... which always brings a certain amount of interest. But also remember that some gentlemen may have ulterior motives, so be cautious and keep your wits about you. Regardless of class or location, men seem to all be alike. Would you not agree?"

I nodded, taking in my aunt's words carefully. "Of course," I said. "Meryton is filled with officers from the militia garrison, I would be a fool to trust them all at their word, would I not?"

Mrs. Gardiner laughed. "Indeed you would be. You are well armed, my dear."

I smiled back at my aunt, but her words were a gentle reminder that not all gentlemen had the best intentions, and that I must be careful with whom I associated.

"There is one gentleman in particular that I would like you to meet," my aunt said, her eyes lighting up. "Mr. Thomas Jackson. His father is a friend of Mr. Gardiner's and I have it on good authority that he is simply charming. He is quite handsome, too."

I arched an eyebrow at my aunt's statement. "Is that so?"

"Indeed," Mrs. Gardiner said with a wink, but then my aunt's expression softened. "Just remember, when you are asked to dance you may, of course, accept or decline as you see fit. Do not feel obligated to dance with anyone that you do not wish to."

I nodded, grateful for my aunt's reassurance.

"And Lizzy," my aunt placed a hand on my arm.

"Remember that you are here to enjoy yourself. I shall keep my opinions to myself unless you ask for them, I do not wish for you to fret too much about the evening that you forget to have fun."

"I will try," I said, managing a small smile.

Just then, there was a knock at the door, and my uncle poked his head into the room. "Do excuse me, Ladies, but the carriage has arrived," he announced with a grin.

My aunt stood and smoothed down the heavy skirts of her ivory satin gown. "Come along, Lizzy. We have a ball to attend."

I stood and followed my aunt down the corridor to the front door. My uncle's valet stood by and bid us a good evening as we retrieved our shawls and reticules from one of the servants who stood nearby.

"It will be a wonderful evening," my aunt said as she kissed my uncle's cheek. "We shall return quite late, dearest."

"As always, I shall stay up to await your homecoming. You know that I am eager to hear all the gossip that I am so often denied."

My aunt laughed and kissed her husband again. "As you command, husband," she said.

My uncle drew her hand to his lips and kissed her gloved knuckles briefly before he turned to me and bid me good evening. "You look beautiful, Lizzy," he said. "Your aunt will have to keep a close watch on you this evening."

"I have already threatened to do so," my aunt cried from the doorway. "Come along, Lizzy!"

"Thank you," I whispered to my uncle and then followed Mrs. Gardener out the door and down the stone steps to where the carriage waited for us.

Deep breaths.

It was only one evening.

And it was only a ball.

I could enjoy myself without any thought of consequences or my own mother harping on every detail of the evening...

I was worried about nothing. My aunt would be there. I would not be alone. And Miss Trainor would be at my side to assist me with meeting new people and learning their names and status...

I would be fine.

TWO
fitzwilliam darcy

ATTENDING YET another London ball was the very last thing I wished to do, but there was no avoiding this one. I had been absent from far too many social engagements during my time in London... and my aunt had begun to notice.

Lady Catherine de Bourgh prided herself on many things—but the most prominent of these virtues was her family name and the power it wielded in London's social circles.

"I have it on good authority that you did not attend Lady Gower's masque last week. I do wonder, Fitzwilliam, if you appreciate the importance of ensuring that you make a prudent match—"

I groaned and pressed my forehead against the window frame.

Behind me, Charles Bingley laughed. "Does she really write to you every week?" he asked incredulously. The sound of paper folding was loud in my ears as Charles tossed the letter onto the desk where I'd tried in vain to hide it.

"She does," I replied through gritted teeth.

Charles' footsteps approached the window, but I could not

look at him. "And she has spies to advise her on which events you have or have not attended?"

I closed my eyes. "She does."

"Miserable," Charles snorted. "She's chosen your bride already, has she not?"

"Probably."

Charles nudged my ribs with his elbow. "You need a drink."

I turned to look at him. "Charles, it's two in the afternoon."

He pointed to the clock. "I think you'll find it's two *thirty* in the afternoon," he said with a sly grin. "High time for a drink."

I let out a heavy sigh. "I suppose."

"Do you have any idea of who it is she has her eye on this time?" Charles asked as he walked to the sideboard. The click of heavy crystal as he poured two glasses of scotch made my shoulders straighten. I wasn't really in the mood for a drink, but holding the glass would be enough.

The weight of it in my hand, the scent of the liquor.

I frowned at the business of the afternoon street below us and then turned to face my friend.

"Several, I'm afraid. But this time... I believe her name is Miss Howard... Miss Howe? I cannot recall..."

Charles snorted and set the stopper back into the decanter. "Miss Georgina Howard is in her seventies," he said.

"Oh..."

Charles held a glass out to me and I took it with some reluctance. "Miss Clarissa Howe, meanwhile, is much younger, and from a much better family."

"How do you know so much about her?"

Charles laughed. "I have, if you recall, two very... knowledgeable sisters."

"Nosy, you mean," I muttered.

Charles lifted his glass in a salute and took a sip of his scotch. "Yes, quite."

"And what do they have to say about her?"

"She is not someone that Caroline would have wished for you to meet, which should tell you much of what you need to know."

I raised my glass to my nose and inhaled the sharpness of the scotch but did not take a drink. My mouth was too dry and a headache loomed behind my eyes. The night ahead was not something I was looking forward to. Lady Blackridge was wealthy and well known in the upper circles of London society. My invitation had been secured by Lady Catherine and there was no way I would be able to avoid it.

Charles clapped me on the back. "Cheer up, old man. It might not be so bad."

"I highly doubt that," I muttered as I leaned against the window sill and stared down at the rain-wet streets.

The thought of being paraded around like a prize horse, forced into conversations with women I had no interest in, and being judged and scrutinized by the entire room made my skin crawl.

But as much as I despised the idea of the ball, I knew I couldn't afford to miss it. Lady Catherine's approval was a powerful tool, and one that I could not afford to lose. I was her heir, after all, and unless my bland cousin was able to secure a match I would be the one to inherit Rosings Park.

I did not doubt that my aunt would do everything in her power to secure a good marriage for Anne... but her first concern seemed to be my own matrimony.

"Well, at the very least you can be certain that Miss Howe is pretty," Charles said encouragingly.

"And how do you know that?"

"Caroline has been heard to remark upon Miss Howe's incredible lack of accomplishment, her terrible singing voice, and how plain she looks in candlelight."

I could not help my chuckle. "If Caroline has nothing but ill words to speak—"

"Then Miss Howe must be a delightful young woman," Charles finished. "I agree. Although, I must warn you—"

My eyebrow rose. "About?"

"Caroline also says that she quite enjoys Miss Howe's company and conversation..."

"Ah."

That was not a good sign. I had been intrigued by Charles' initial report, but if Miss Howe and Caroline Bingley had an affinity—that could be nothing more than a warning. Caroline was notoriously waspish and backbiting, and the only young women she had a kind word for were those who were just as tedious and dangerous as she.

I would have to keep my wits about me, that much was certain.

* * *

AS I STOOD in front of the mirror, adjusting my neck cloth for what felt like the hundredth time, I couldn't help but feel a sense of dread wash over me. The ballroom was filled to the brim with the most eligible young ladies in London and their equally ambitious mothers, all vying for a chance to secure a good match.

I wasn't a stranger to these social circles, but I had always found all of this... nonsense... to be an endless parade of superficiality and pretense. My aunt, of course, believed differently.

I scanned the room, taking in the sea of faces and tried my best to pick out any familiar ones. The musicians played with elegant enthusiasm in one corner of the room and the dance floor took up much of the space in the ballroom.

Lady Blackridge was much more fond of dancing than she

was anything else, and I knew that the dances would continue until almost dawn.

I could only hope that I would be gone long before that.

Charles had pointed out Miss Clarissa Howe when we had arrived, and I was careful to keep a watchful eye upon her as we moved about the room. But Charles had abandoned me to dance and my nerves had begun to creep upon me once more.

Miss Howe was surrounded by a gaggle of young women who were giggling and whispering amongst themselves. Caroline Bingley and Louisa Hurst were nearby, and I could observe how close a watch Caroline kept upon the other young woman.

As Charles had said, Miss Howe was beautiful—quite the opposite of Caroline's assessment, as I had suspected. But there was something about her that I did not quite trust. Perhaps it was the tilt of her head when she observed the other young ladies who passed by—or the way the other women with her reacted to whatever it was they were speaking about. Almost as though they were afraid of her... Whatever it was, I did not like it.

But my main adversary that evening was Mrs. Loreen Howe. If I could get through the evening without being cornered by Miss Howe's formidable mother, I might be able to avoid an introduction altogether—but it seemed as though fate had other plans.

I felt a tap on my shoulder and turned to face a woman who was unmistakably Mrs. Loreen Howe. She had a face like a bulldog, an expensive yet gaudy gown in an unflattering shade of pink, and a voice that grated on my nerves.

"Mr. Darcy, how delightful to see you here tonight," she said with a smile that did not reach her eyes. "I have been wanting to introduce you to my daughter, Miss Clarissa Howe. I do hope you will find her company to your liking. Your esteemed aunt seemed to think that you would be well matched... and I would flatter myself to agree with her assessment."

I forced a polite smile onto my face and inclined my head in her direction. "It would be my pleasure, Mrs. Howe."

She gestured to her daughter, who was still surrounded by her coterie of friends. "Clarissa, dear, you must come and meet Mr. Darcy."

Miss Howe turned to face me, and I was taken aback by the intensity of her gaze. Her pale blue eyes seemed to look straight through me, and a shiver ran down my spine. But I kept my composure and offered her a small bow.

"Mr. Darcy, it is a pleasure to make your acquaintance," she said, her voice soft yet commanding. "I have heard so much about you from my dear friend Miss Caroline Bingley."

I raised an eyebrow as my stomach sank. If Caroline had been speaking about me to Miss Howe, it could not be for any good reason. The young lady's smile widened, and I realized that she was waiting for me to say something.

"Is that so?" I asked, keeping my voice neutral.

Miss Howe nodded and her smile took on a more catlike appearance. I could see why Caroline felt threatened by her. She was beautiful in a cold way, and calculating—very certainly.

"She speaks very highly of you, Mr. Darcy," Miss Howe continued. "She says that, as well as being a man of great wealth and influence, that you are also in possession of impeccable taste and manners."

I suppressed a grimace. Caroline was clearly trying to set us up, and I had no interest in being a pawn in her games.

"Caroline is too kind," I said, my tone clipped.

Miss Howe's smile faltered slightly, but she quickly recovered. "Oh, but I cannot agree with you, sir. Miss Bingley always speaks the truth, no matter how unpleasant it may be. And I have come to learn that she is always right about people."

I couldn't help but feel a sense of unease at her words. It was clear that Miss Howe and Caroline had a close relationship, and I did not trust Caroline's judgment in the slightest. But I knew I had to be careful not to offend Miss Howe or her mother, as Lady Catherine would not take kindly to any affronts towards their family.

"Of course, Miss Howe," I said with a polite nod. "I look forward to getting to know you better this evening."

As we made small talk, I couldn't help but feel as though I was being studied under a microscope. Miss Howe's gaze never left my face, and I could feel her assessing me with every word I spoke. It was unnerving, to say the least.

"Do you dance, Mr. Darcy?" Mrs. Howe asked suddenly.

"I—"

"Darcy, there you are!" Charles Bingley's jovial voice broke through the noise of the conversation around us and I could have laughed with relief. "You must come at once!"

"Ladies," I said quickly. "You must forgive me— I shall return with all haste."

"See that you do, Mr. Darcy," Mrs. Howe said with a frown. Her fan fluttered angrily and I could see disdain in her daughter's pale blue eyes, but I did not care.

Charles and I bowed hastily to the ladies and I allowed my friend to lead me back through the crowd.

"Whatever is the matter?" I asked.

"You looked like you were in need of saving," Charles said with a grin.

I shook my head, trying to rid myself of the memory of Miss Howe's intense gaze. "Thank you, Charles. That woman—"

"Mrs. Howe?" Charles asked, his expression suddenly serious. "What did she say to you?"

"Introduced me to her daughter, as my aunt intended, I suppose," I said with a shrug. "Miss Howe was very clear about her friendship with Caroline and mentioned that your sister had spoken highly of me. Nothing of consequence."

Charles frowned. "I was not aware that they were such close friends... But you know Caroline— she's always up to something."

"I'm well aware," I said, feeling an undercurrent of annoyance. I didn't like being maneuvered like a pawn in someone else's game. It was bad enough that my aunt was so invested in my romantic life, I didn't need Caroline Bingley's intervention as well—especially as I knew that I couldn't trust it. Her own interest in me had been more than obvious in the past few years, but I didn't have the heart to be cruel to her as would have been necessary to keep her away for good.

We reached a quieter corner of the room, where we could speak more freely. "What did you need me for?" I asked.

Charles hesitated for a moment before speaking. "I know you do not need any other distractions this evening," he said. "But I have met a young lady—"

I could not help but laugh. "Have you?"

"It's not what you think," Charles huffed. "She is from Hertfordshire."

"Oh?" The name of the place was familiar, though I could not place why that might be.

Charles let out an exasperated sigh. "How do you not recall this?"

The only response I had was a blank stare.

"Mr. Barrow, my solicitor, mentioned a house that was available in Hertfordshire. A lovely country estate completed with a forest for riding and even a herd of deer—Darcy, really?"

"I—" And then it came to me. He had spoken of the place endlessly without even seeing more than an illustration of the house and a stack of faded building plans. "Netherferry—"

"Nether*field* Park," Charles groaned.

"Netherfield. Of course. I did not forget," I said in a rush. "What of it?"

"She *knows* it," Charles said through gritted teeth. "The estate. She knows it very well, it is only three miles from her own estate." He was clearly frustrated with me, but there was nothing I could do about that.

"And who is this young woman?"

Charles pointed toward the dance floor. "There, with dark hair, in the lilac gown."

I found her at once. She was the only young lady in lilac while all the others were dressed in ivory and shades of pink and pale blue. As I watched her dance, I couldn't help but notice the way she moved with such grace and ease.

Her partner, a tall and lanky gentleman with sandy hair, seemed to be struggling to keep up with her.

I couldn't help but think how out of place she looked—her simple yet elegant gown was a refreshing contrast to the somewhat overwrought styles that the other young ladies wore.

"Who is she?" I asked, turning back to Charles.

"Her name is Miss Elizabeth Bennet. She's the second eldest daughter of a gentleman in Hertfordshire," Charles said. "She's quite unlike any other lady I've met before."

I raised an eyebrow. Charles had a way of losing his heart before his mind had a chance to catch up with him. He had disappointed many a young lady in recent years, much to his elder sister's dismay, and Caroline's amusement. "In what way?"

"She's intelligent, for one," Charles said, a smile spreading across his face. "And she has a wit that rivals even yours, my friend."

I couldn't help but feel intrigued.

Intelligence and wit were qualities I admired greatly in a woman, and it was rare to find someone who possessed both in addition to a pretty face. Elizabeth Bennet, it seemed, was a rare bird among a flock of London pigeons.

"Well, I suppose I shall have to meet her then," I said. "The dance is just ending. Shall we go over?"

The musicians played the final notes of the dance and we waited to the side as the dancers resumed their places and bowed to their partners. Miss Bennet's lanky partner seemed out of breath, but Miss Bennet seemed unbothered by the exercise.

As we made our way over to where Miss Bennet was standing, I couldn't help but feel a sense of excitement building within me. Despite myself, I was eager to see if she lived up to Charles' description.

As we approached, Miss Bennet turned to face us, her dark eyes met mine for just a moment before she glanced away. A bright smile crossed her face as she recognized Charles. She curtsied politely, and I found myself captivated by the way she held herself—with a quiet confidence that was both alluring and refreshing.

"Mr. Bingley," she exclaimed. "I did not expect to see you so soon."

"Miss Bennet," Charles said with a broad smile, "may I introduce my good friend Mr. Darcy, I spoke about him earlier."

Not again.

Why did everyone have to speak about me to young ladies?

"I shall say now that Darcy is very pleased to make your acquaintance, though his face does not show it," Charles said as he nudged his elbow into my ribs.

Very funny.

"Miss Bennet, I wonder if you could, once more, tell me about Netherfield Park," Charles said. "Darcy does not believe how passionate I am about this estate."

Miss Bennet's dark eyes flickered to mine, her delicate brow lifted in amusement. "Perhaps Mr. Darcy does not appreciate the country as you do," she said.

"Oh, quite the contrary," Charles laughed. "Darcy has his own estate to worry about in Derbyshire. He knows the countryside very well, in fact it is because of Pemberley that I am seeking an estate of my own—I fancy myself more of a country gentleman than anything."

"And you, Mr. Darcy, is that where your passions lie as well?" she asked.

I blinked at her in surprise. "I— That is to say— Of course—"

"Netherfield is, of course, nothing to Pemberley," Charles continued unabated. "But I do long for a quiet life away from the rush and noise of the city."

"Your wife is similarly minded?" Elizabeth asked him, but her eyes were on me.

Sly creature. How very clever to ask such a thing.

"Ah, sadly I am not in possession of such a treasure," Charles said. "But it would be a rare thing to discover a young lady who might be in possession of a similar fondness for such a life."

"Indeed," Elizabeth said with a smile.

I COULDN'T HELP but feel a sense of admiration for Miss Bennet as she and Charles began to discuss Netherfield Park. She did, indeed, know the estate well and described it with an accuracy that made me recall the plans Charles had shown me with more clarity.

Her intelligence and wit were not just for show, and she possessed a charm and grace that was truly captivating. As we continued to converse, I found myself drawn to her effortless beauty and the ease with which she carried herself.

It was a rare quality, one that I had not seen in any other young lady in London.

"Darcy," Charles said suddenly. "You and Miss Bennet must dance. I insist upon it."

I was about to question Charles' outburst when I realized the direction of his gaze.

Mrs. Howe was making her way toward us through the crowd, and she did not look pleased. Her daughter followed behind in the wake she made as she pushed through the other guests and I did not like the look upon her face, either.

"Indeed," I said quickly. "A grand idea. Miss Bennet? If you are willing?"

"Am I saving you from a terrible fate?" she asked as she glanced over my shoulder.

"You certainly are," Charles answered for me. "My sister, and Darcy's aunt, believes that the young lady approaching us is the very best match for Darcy—an opinion which no one else agrees with."

"Oh, dear," Miss Bennet murmured. "I suppose I shall have to save you."

THREE
elizabeth

THE GENTLEMAN'S dark eyes were pleading as he swallowed hard. "Please, Miss Bennet," he whispered.

"I cannot refuse to help someone in need," I said quickly and held out my hand. "You are very kind, Mr. Darcy," I said louder so that the people standing nearby could hear me. "I would love to dance."

Mr. Darcy took my hand and led me onto the dance floor. As we stepped into position and the music began, I couldn't help but feel a sense of anticipation. Despite my initial reservations about Mr. Darcy's aloofness, I found myself intrigued by him. His strong build and confident demeanor were certainly appealing, but it was his intelligence and wit that had me truly captivated.

"So, Mr. Darcy," I began, unable to resist teasing him a little. "Do you always let your friend dictate your dance partners?"

He raised an eyebrow in surprise, but a small smile tugged at the corners of his lips. "Certainly not always. But in this particular instance, I am grateful for Charles' meddling."

I chuckled at his response, delighted to see a glimpse of humor in his eyes.

"You are quite the dancer," he said, his voice low and smooth as we moved across the floor.

"As are you," I replied, enjoying the warmth of his hand in mine. "And who was the young lady you were so eager to escape?"

"No one of any consequence," he replied quickly.

I glanced toward the edge of the dance floor where the formidably broad woman and her elegant daughter stood at the edge of the crowd. The young woman glared at the dancers, and specifically at me and I looked away.

"Ah, I see," I said, trying not to let my curiosity get the better of me. "Well, I am glad we were able to avoid any unpleasantness."

"Indeed," he murmured, his gaze fixed on me. "Miss Bennet, I must ask...what is it about the countryside that you so enjoy?"

I smiled, feeling a warmth spread through me at the question. "Oh, where to begin? The fresh air, the open spaces, the quiet... I must admit that I do find it all so invigorating. There is something about being surrounded by nature that makes me feel alive."

He listened intently as I spoke, and I could sense a shared appreciation for the beauty of nature and the peace of the countryside. As the dance came to an end, I found myself feeling a sense of disappointment. I wanted to continue talking with Mr. Darcy, to explore this newfound connection we seemed to have.

"Thank you for the dance," he said, bowing politely. "I must say, I have greatly enjoyed our conversation."

I smiled, feeling a flutter in my chest at his words. "As have I, Mr. Darcy. Perhaps we could continue it another time?"

He hesitated for just a moment before nodding. "There is no need to stop now," he said. "Shall we have another?"

I could not stop my smile as his dark eyes met mine. "Indeed, I cannot see why we should not."

* * *

AS THE EVENING wound to a close, I found that I had lost count of the times that Mr. Darcy had invited me to the dance floor.

The dark-eyed young woman had watched us with intensity for a few dances, but then she had melted into the crowd and I lost sight of her. Mr. Bingley danced with me once or twice and his excitable conversation was bent with sincere singularity upon Netherfield Park. His personality was jovial and bright, and I wondered if he might be a good match for my sister Jane. Her quiet manners might soothe him, and his effervescence might bring her own shining personality forth... It was a possibility that I would have to spend more time cultivating.

Especially if he was to make an offer for the estate. Only time would tell.

"Mr. Bingley, who was the young lady that Mr. Darcy was avoiding earlier?" I asked as Mr. Bingley took my hand for a final dance.

The gentleman had the good sense to look somewhat chagrined as he glanced over his shoulder to where his friend stood at the edge of the dancers.

"Miss Clarissa Howe," he said in a voice so low I had to struggle to hear him over the sound of the music.

"And who is she?"

Charles' gaze darted around the room before he met my eyes once more. "She will not hear you," I reassured him.

His smile was nervous. "Be that as it may— Darcy's aunt, Lady Catherine de Bourgh has taken a great interest in his marital status... especially as he currently has none. Miss Clarissa Howe seems to be her best attempt to change that fact."

"I see," I said. "And yet, he has not danced with her at all tonight."

Charles Bingley shook his head. "Indeed, not."

I tried to ignore the twinge of jealousy in my chest and tried to keep a smile upon my face and my voice light. "Does Mr. Darcy disagree with his aunt's choice?"

Mr. Bingley laughed shortly. "He certainly does not."

"A pity," I murmured.

"He seems to have been otherwise occupied tonight," Mr. Bingley said. His smile was warm and I glanced over to the edge of the dance floor where Mr. Darcy waited.

Was he waiting to ask me to dance again?

I would not say no if he did.

But as the dance came to an end, I caught sight of my aunt, who stood with Miss Lily Trainor. Their expressions were unexpectedly worried... and my throat tightened as the final notes of the dance played. I was so distracted that I missed one of my steps, but Mr. Bingley adjusted his own movements to hide my mistake from anyone who might have been watching.

"Are you quite all right?" he murmured.

"Fine, I thank you," I replied. "My shoe..." It was a lame excuse, but I had been dancing all evening and from my aunt's worried countenance, I had a feeling that it was time I attended to other matters than my own enjoyment of the ball.

"Thank you for the dances," I said. "You have been a gracious partner."

"I look forward to seeing you in Hertfordshire," Mr. Bingley replied. "Perhaps you might introduce me to your sister?"

"Indeed I shall," I said with a smile.

He bowed as I curtsied and then extended his elbow to escort me back to the edge of the crowd.

I introduced Mr. Bingley to my aunt, but the gentleman took his leave soon after, and as he disappeared into the crowd I found myself wondering where Mr. Darcy had gone... It struck me then, the reality of our situation. He was a man of means, and I was the daughter of a country gentleman in Hertfordshire.

Our paths would likely never cross again.

"Lizzy," my aunt said, "we must leave at once."

Her voice was low, and she seemed nervous though her back was straight and she kept a smile upon her face. Miss Trainor, however, was not having similar success in keeping her features neutral.

I could not leave without knowing what was happening. "What is it?"

"You have been upon the dance floor, and we could not interrupt," Lily Trainor hissed. "But there are rumors—people are talking—"

"How many times did you dance with Mr. Darcy?" my aunt asked.

"I— I do not know."

My aunt's lips pressed into a thin line. "Never mind now," she said. "Come, the carriage is waiting."

I did not ask any other questions, but followed my aunt through the ballroom and out into the foyer of the Blackridge's grand house.

As we stepped out into the cool night air, I noticed that there was only one carriage waiting in the courtyard. My aunt hurried me toward it with Miss Trainor following close behind.

"What is going on?" I asked, my heart pounding in my chest. "Why must we leave?"

My aunt said nothing and stepped up into the carriage as soon as the footman opened the door. I took the man's hand to step up into the carriage and settled myself into the plush seat opposite my aunt.

Confusion swept through me as Miss Trainor clambered up beside me and the carriage door slammed shut. The sound made me jump and I stared out the window at the house—every window was ablaze with candlelight and I regretted that we had to leave so quickly—I had not even been able to bid Mr. Darcy goodnight...

As the carriage jolted forward and began to move through the crowded streets, I was finally able to gather my thoughts.

"You must tell me what is happening," I said. "Did something—"

"There were rumors," Lily said. "Vicious and spiteful ones."

"Did you say anything to anyone?" Mrs. Gardiner asked. "Anything that might have been taken as an insult or an affront..."

I stared at my aunt incredulously. "I beg your pardon?"

"No, I thought not," she said ruefully.

"You said nothing to Miss Clarissa Howe?" Lily's question was breathless.

"No— Indeed, I did not even meet her," I replied.

"Oh, dear."

I had had almost enough of this mysterious talk. "Come now," I said. "Speak plainly. I was having a perfectly lovely time—"

"Lizzy, you were the talk of the ball," my aunt said softly. "But not in a way that I might have wished."

My throat tightened. "I beg your pardon?"

"Your reputation— It was..."

"It was called into question," Lily interrupted. "Multiple times... and no one knew you and so it was easier to take the word of whoever had spoken— Before long it was the only topic of discussion..."

I looked at my aunt as desperation clawed at my chest. Mrs. Gardiner smiled in a manner that I interpreted as an attempt at reassurance, but I did not feel comforted in the slightest.

"You must not worry," my aunt said, but her tone was

strange. "It will not matter. The people who gossip here in London do not do it anywhere else."

"But— you are my aunt, surely they will talk about you as well," I ventured as the carriage turned another corner.

Mrs. Gardiner let out a choked laugh. "Let them try," she said. "Lady Blackridge knows better than to listen to Mrs. Loreen Howe."

"But do the others?" Lily Trainor's eyes were wide. "I do not like it," she said. "Whatever you did to anger Miss Howe, you should write her an apology at once."

The carriage pulled to a stop and bounced slightly as the footman jumped down to open the door to allow Lily to clamber down.

"I will send your gown in the morning," I said as she stepped down into the street.

"Keep it," Lily replied. Her smile was faint. "I shall never be able to wear it again for fear of association... If anyone sees that gown again, they will think of you at once! No, no, take it away with you to the countryside where it shall never be seen again."

She was trying to be amusing, but her words only left me feeling cold. "Thank you," I said, but she had already turned to flee toward the stairs that led up to her house.

I sat back in my seat as the carriage door closed and the carriage lurched into motion once more.

Mrs. Gardiner leaned across to lay her hand upon mine. "Do not worry," she said. "I promise that this will all come to nothing. Some petty jealousy, I am certain of it. I shall get to the bottom of it. But you needn't worry."

"No, I suppose not," I murmured.

But why would Miss Howe, a young lady I had never met, have such an ill will toward me?

FOUR
darcy

FOR A FORTNIGHT AFTER THE BALL, I found myself haunted by thoughts of Miss Elizabeth Bennet. I could not shake the memory of her grace and beauty, nor could I forget the way her dark eyes had met mine as we danced... or how different she was to every other young lady I'd ever met.

Different from every other young lady that Lady Catherine de Bourgh wished to turn into Mrs. Darcy.

No, I was tired of the games and the arrangements. They had to stop.

My aunt was, of course, infuriated with me. By her estimation, I should have been halfway to engaged. But I was very far from that.

Very far, indeed.

And for a fortnight I had tried to avoid Miss Clarissa Howe.

My aunt's insistence on the young lady seemed to have given her mother a certain, unearned, status among the upper circles of London society and I was updated on her movements with more frequency than I might have liked by Caroline Bingley.

Seated in the drawing room as I attempted to write a letter

to my sister, who was , of course, eager for news of our friends in the city, Caroline sighed as she paced in front of the window in an attempt to draw my attention.

"What is it, Caroline," Charles asked in a bored tone. I glanced over at my friend, but he had not looked up from his newspaper.

"I was simply wondering when I might be able to invite my friends over to tea," she began.

"Why would you not be able to do such a thing?" Charles wasn't actually interested in what his sister had to say, but not engaging in conversation was a dangerous thing when Caroline was involved.

"I would not risk it when there is a chance that my friends might feel—uncomfortable in my home," she replied sweetly.

Charles looked up at his sister. "And what the blazes do you mean by that?"

Caroline's smile was saccharine sweet as she turned away from the window to meet his stare. "Why, nothing, of course, Charles. It is only that Miss Howe does not wish to be somewhere that she is not wanted—even though it was made very clear that she *was* welcome."

"Caroline, say what you mean," Charles snapped. "My head aches with your scheming."

"I believe Mr. Darcy knows very well what I mean," she said. "Do you not?"

"Miss Howe is laboring under the impression that she would be engaged to Darcy by the end of the month," Charles said. "Is that right?"

Caroline's lips pressed into a thin line. "Laboring is not the term I would use," she said primly. "I have it on good authority that Lady Catherine de Bourgh herself made this match. And what would you know about it, Charles?"

"I know that her Ladyship does not have any idea what

she's doing when it comes to matchmaking," Charles said firmly.

Caroline's eyes widened. "Charles—"

"I've had enough of this," he said. He folded his newspaper with an authoritative *snap* and stood. "Invite whomsoever you like to tea, Darcy and I are leaving London."

"Oh, indeed?" Caroline retorted. "And where are you going?"

"To Hertfordshire," he said.

I had never seen my friend behave in such a manner when speaking to his elder sister, and I was impressed by it.

Caroline, for her part, looked shocked at this sudden change in his demeanor. "And when will you return?"

"Whenever we please," Charles replied. "Come along, Darcy. We have an appointment and must not be late."

I set aside my quill and tucked my half-written letter into my ledger. Charles deposited his newspaper upon a side table and strode from the room without another word and I pushed my chair back from the desk and followed him.

"Mr. Darcy," Caroline said.

I paused at the doorway, even though I knew that I should not have. "Yes?"

"It really is quite cruel of you to ignore Miss Howe," she said smoothly. "She really is quite a beauty, and very accomplished."

"I'm sure," I said. "Good day, Caroline."

"You're making a mistake," she called after me. "Surely, you can see it. She will be wanting to speak to you when you return from your little jaunt in the countryside."

"Indeed," I muttered as I turned and walked into the corridor to catch up with Charles. Whatever my friend's plans were did not matter to me. Escaping Caroline and the looming threat of Miss Clarissa Howe was infinitely more appealing.

Charles was already in the foyer and his valet was helping him into his coat.

"Where are we going?" I hissed as I handed my ledger to the footman who appeared to assist me.

"To see my solicitor," he replied with a grin. "I was very serious when I said that we were going to Hertfordshire. I plan to make a visit to Netherfield Park and you shall accompany me to give me your opinion on the place."

The possibility that I might see Miss Elizabeth Bennet again made my spine straighten just a little. "Is that so?"

Charles' eyebrow rose. "Will I be taking you away from your business here in London?"

Considering that my only business in London seemed to go hand-in-hand with an engagement to a young lady I did not wish to become acquainted with, I was happy to leave.

"No, indeed," I said as I shrugged into my coat. I thanked the footman and took my hat from his hands. "When do you wish to depart?"

"In the morning, I should think," he said. "I have had Mr. Barrow working on this little excursion since the day after Lady Blackridge's ball. It is high time that I made this little dream of mine come true."

"Indeed," I murmured.

Charles flung open the front door and rushed down the stone steps to the street.

Raining. Of course.

I shoved my hat onto my head and headed out into the early spring morning. Charles was on a mission, and I was apparently coming with him. The only other choice was to stay behind at the house and await the arrival of Caroline's horrid friends, which would no doubt include a certain young lady that I did not wish to speak to.

I knew that I could not avoid Miss Clarissa Howe forever,

but first I had to decide how to extricate myself from the situation that my aunt had forced me into.

I needed time to plan... or, at the very least, stay out of sight until Caroline had found something new to be enraged about.

* * *

"ARE you certain that this is what you want?"

I had asked Charles this very same question no less than four times, but every time his answer was the same.

"With every fiber of my being."

It was difficult not to be swept up in Charles' excitement about Netherfield Park. My own estate had come to me through my father's death... and there had been nothing joyous about it. I wondered if I might feel differently if I were to acquire an estate on my own merits... Perhaps I would feel the same sort of exuberance that had recently overwhelmed Charles' sensibilities.

He had never been a stoic-minded sort of gentleman, but any hint of that mindset had been forgotten in the face of what lay ahead of him. I did not know what sort of life he pictured for himself at Netherfield Park, but I did not wish to dampen his spirits with the realities of his new position.

Charles wanted to ride to Hertfordshire—it was not a terrible hardship, and the cool spring weather was ideal for riding. Our trunks would be sent by carriage, and Charles was so eager to depart that we set out straight from the solicitor's office.

WE RODE in silence for some time, our horses' hooves pounding a steady rhythm on the earth. The mist hung low around us, shrouding the countryside in a soft, hazy light. In the distance, I could see the outline of a grand house, rising up out of the landscape like a beacon.

It was Netherfield Park.

As we drew closer, I could see that the house was grander than I had anticipated.

Its towering facade was made of honey-colored stone, and tall windows glinted in the sun. The front lawn was neatly manicured, and a fountain bubbled merrily in the center of a circular drive. Charles let out a low whistle of appreciation.

"By Jove," he said. "Isn't she a beauty?"

"She certainly is," I replied.

"It's nothing to Pemberley, of course," Charles blurted out.

"Nonsense, it is well situated in a pleasing aspect, and it is everything you hoped that it would be, is it not?"

Charles' grin was answer enough, but I could not deny that seeing Netherfield up close made me long to return to Derbyshire and my own estate.

We tethered our horses at the stables and made our way up to the house. The door was opened by a plump, smiling house-keeper, who ushered us in with a flurry of curtsies.

"Oh, Mr. Bingley, we've been expecting you for some days now," she exclaimed. "Won't you come into the parlor?"

We followed the housekeeper down the corridor, and I trailed a few steps behind to take in the decor. As we entered the room, I couldn't help but notice that the furniture was worn, and the walls were in need of a fresh coat of paint. However, the room was still tastefully decorated, and I could see that Charles was pleased with what he saw.

"It's perfect," Charles said, turning to me with a grin.

"I'm glad to hear it," I said, offering him a small smile.

"If you'll wait here— I'll fetch some tea."

"It's marvelous, isn't it?" Charles exclaimed.

"It is... something."

We had not been waiting long when a door opened, and a young woman entered the room. She was tall and slender, with fair hair that curled in soft waves around her face. She wore a simple muslin gown and a smile that was both warm and welcoming.

"Mr. Bingley," she said, extending her hand. "I am Miss Jane Bennet. You are very welcome to Netherfield Park."

"Miss Bennet," Charles exclaimed. "I am very pleased to meet you— But I was expecting—"

"Mr. Jarret, I know," she replied. "He was unable to come to meet you today, he has taken quite ill."

I knew that Charles had been quite keen to meet with the caretaker he had been exchanging letters with for the last few months, and I could see the disappointment in his expression— but also how quickly it was replaced by delight at seeing Miss Bennet.

"Oh, that is a shame," Charles said.

"We are told that he will recover in time," she replied. "But, in his absence, he has asked my sister and I to accompany you on a tour of the house."

As she spoke, Elizabeth Bennet stepped into the parlor. She, too, wore a plain muslin dress, but she was just as beautiful as the night I had danced with her in London. Her cheeks were pink and her smile was bright, though I sensed that there was something amiss when she looked in my direction.

Was she angry with me for not bidding her goodnight at the ball? I had tried to find her, but was informed that she had departed with haste— Caroline had seemed particularly amused by it, but I had not pried further as Miss Howe had been mentioned soon after...

I would have to speak with her and apologize... Surely, I would be forgiven.

"Mr. Bingley, would you and your friend—"

"Mr. Darcy," Elizabeth said, "that is his name."

Jane Bennet's eyes narrowed briefly, but then she smiled once more. "Of course. Gentlemen, if you would come with us?"

Charles glanced at me in surprise, but I could do nothing but shrug in response.

We followed the Bennet sisters through the house, admiring the grandeur and charm of Netherfield Park. As we made our way up to the second floor, Elizabeth and I fell back from the rest of the group.

"I hope that you can forgive my absence at the end of the ball, Miss Bennet," I said, breaking the silence between us. "I had intended to bid you goodnight, but it seemed that you had already departed."

Elizabeth's cheeks flushed, and she looked away from me. "I...it was nothing, Mr. Darcy. My aunt was feeling unwell and we departed with haste."

"How unfortunate, I do hope it was not serious?"

"No, indeed. She was quite recovered the following morning."

"I see," I replied, feeling a twinge of disappointment. Perhaps our encounter at the ball had meant more to me than it had to her.

We continued walking in silence until we reached a large bedroom with a four-poster bed and large windows that overlooked the gardens. Jane Bennet turned to us with a smile.

"While you are Mr. Jarret's guests, this room will be Mr. Bingley's," she said. "And Mr. Darcy, you will be staying in the guest room across the corridor."

"Thank you, Miss Bennet," I said, with a nod.

"How long do you intend to stay?" Elizabeth asked.

Charles' grin was wide. "A fortnight at the very least," he said. "Although I would venture to say that it may be longer. At Mr. Jarrett's pleasure, of course. My solicitor—"

"I'm sure everything is in order," Jane replied. "There will be servants to assist you, and the kitchen is well staffed."

"Delightful," Charles exclaimed. "Charming and delightful."

As we made our way out of the room, Elizabeth turned to me. "I hope that you will enjoy your stay in Hertfordshire, Mr. Darcy. I assure you, my sister and I will do our best to make you feel welcome."

"I have no doubt of that, Miss Bennet," I replied, unable to resist the urge to reach out and touch her arm. "And I look forward to getting to know you better."

Elizabeth's eyes widened at my touch, but she did not pull away. Instead, she smiled politely and nodded before quickly making her way down the hallway to catch up with her sister.

"Come along, gentlemen," Jane called out. "We shall see the rest of the house, and then the grounds."

I exchanged a glance with Charles. He seemed overjoyed with each new thing that we saw, and I knew that he was not looking closely at the details of the house—or all of the repairs and maintenance that would need to be undertaken to bring the house up to a standard that would be required for comfort.

"What do you think?" Charles hissed as we followed the Bennet sisters down the stairs toward the main corridor.

"The house? There are some repairs needed, to be sure—"

"No— About Miss Jane Bennet!"

"Oh—"

"I daresay she is the most beautiful woman I have ever laid eyes on."

"She is very pretty—"

Jane Bennet was beautiful, but my eyes were drawn back each time to her sister.

Her lack of fortune and connections held no interest for me. I had grown tired of my aunt's insistence that such things were of any importance at all. There was something about Elizabeth Bennet that drew me to her.

Perhaps it was her wit, her intelligence, or her fine eyes and the way they sparkled in the spring sunshine.

Or perhaps it was simply her spirit of independence that I found so intriguing.

Whatever the reason, I knew that I wanted to spend more time with her. As we walked with the Bennet sisters through Netherfield Park's grounds and admired the ancient roses that climbed the arbor, I made a decision.

I would stay at Netherfield Park for as long as it took to win Elizabeth Bennet's heart.

FIVE
elizabeth

"IS that the Mr. Darcy you spoke of," Jane whispered as we took the path toward Netherfield Park's stables.

"The very same," I replied softly.

"He seems not to know that anything is amiss," she said.

"No, indeed not."

"Then you must believe that the rumors were all unfounded," Jane insisted. "Surely, as a gentleman who was accused of such things would not march into your presence without so much as an apology—or a sense of shame!"

"He did apologize," I said.

Jane stared at me. "He did?"

I nodded. "He apologized that he was not able to bid me goodnight at Lady Blackridge's ball."

"Oh... But what does that mean?"

"It means that our aunt's suspicions were correct," I said. "Although, I believe I should confront the gentleman and discover the truth of it from his own lips."

"Oh, Lizzy, are you certain—"

"I am."

"Ladies, are you certain that this is the correct path?"

Mr. Bingley let out a frustrated grunt as a branch struck him in the chest.

"Indeed, it is," Jane sang out. "Mr. Jarrett did apologize that the stables have not been kept to the same standard as they ought to be—but a simple afternoon's work should set them right again!"

"What do you think of Mr. Bingley?" I asked as I glanced back at the gentleman who we had left to struggle through the underbrush.

"He's very handsome," Jane said. "And quite entertaining to speak with."

"I told you as much, did I not?"

"You did," Jane said. Her cheeks were flushed and she looked back over her shoulder again. "I should like to get to know him better, I think."

"You should," I said with a smile. "I did enjoy his company at the ball. He is a wonderful dancer, if a little... enthusiastic."

Jane's eyes were bright as she laughed. "Then let us hope that they stay at Netherfield long enough to attend one of the assemblies..."

"Indeed," I replied.

As we arrived at the stables, Jane and Mr. Bingley walked on ahead and I waited for Mr. Darcy to catch up.

"Miss Bennet," he said with a nod. "I must thank you for coming to do this, Mr. Jarrett was right to ask you to lead this tour. You know this estate very well, indeed."

I inclined my head, my thoughts racing... How was I to begin this— "May I have a word with you, Mr. Darcy?" I blurted out.

"Of course," he replied, his expression giving nothing away.

I led him away from the others, towards a small copse of trees where we could speak privately. Mr. Darcy followed me silently.

"Whatever can it be that you would wish—"

"I wish to speak with you about the rumors that have been circulating about your character," I said, crossing my arms. "I believe that as a gentleman, you are obligated to address them."

Mr. Darcy's expression remained neutral. "And what rumors would those be, Miss Bennet?"

"Rumors that have stained my own reputation," I said hotly. "That you have been engaging in... inappropriate conduct with women in London," I said, my voice trembling slightly. "My aunt was quite certain of it. And so were all of the ladies at the ball. My aunt could not show herself in polite society for weeks, and a young woman I thought was my friend would not speak to me afterward! She would not even allow me to return the gown I had borrowed. It is still in my wardrobe and I cannot wear it because it is too fine for Meryton society!"

I had not meant to say all of that, but I could not stop myself. My cheeks were hot and I felt lightheaded, but it was strangely freeing to be able to release some of the tension that I had been feeling.

"I see," Mr. Darcy said slowly. "I had no idea— All of this because we..."

"We danced far too many dances at the ball," I said quickly.

It sounded ridiculous to say it aloud, but that was the heart of the matter.

"And do you believe these rumors to be true, Miss Bennet?"

"I cannot say," I admitted. "That is why I wished to speak with you about it. I cannot judge your character without hearing your side of the story. And I thought it only fair that you should know— That was why we departed so suddenly."

"Not a sudden illness?"

I shook my head.

Mr. Darcy studied me for a long moment before speaking. "Miss Bennet , I can assure you that those rumors are false. I have never engaged in any such behavior and I take my reputation very seriously."

I relaxed slightly at his words. "I am glad to hear it, Mr. Darcy."

He nodded. "I am sorry that you fell victim to such rumors — I do hope they have not affected you?"

I shook my head. "No, indeed. The only advantage to living outside of London is that I needn't trouble myself with London gossip. Although, I do worry that there is a certain young lady behind all of these horrible things that have been said—"

The gentleman's jaw tightened. "Indeed... She shall not trouble you here, and I promise that as soon as I return to London that I shall speak to her about this behavior. It is unbecoming of a young lady of her station."

I looked up at him, studying his face. It was a passable apology, but it did not change anything about what had been said about me. If I were a young lady living in London I would be in perpetual fear of my reputation, but I was safe here in Hertfordshire... Perhaps this was enough. He had promised to speak to the young lady, Miss Howe, perhaps that would be the end of it.

There was also something in his eyes that made me want to believe that he could correct this injustice, and also made me want to trust him.

"I will keep an open mind, Mr. Darcy," I said at last. "But I hope you understand that it will take more than just words to convince me."

"I understand," he said. "And I am willing to do whatever it takes to prove my character to you."

I nodded. "Thank you, Mr. Darcy. I appreciate your honesty."

As we walked back towards the stables, I couldn't help but feel that spark of attraction that I had first experienced at the ball... There was something about him that drew me to him, but I could not be certain if it was wise to feel such a thing.

Not yet.

* * *

THE TOUR of Netherfield Park was more exhilarating than I could have expected, and when we finally bid the gentlemen a good day, Jane and I were both exhausted.

"I could have spent hours more in Mr. Bingley's company," Jane sighed as we walked back toward the road that would lead us home to Longbourn.

"I believe Mr. Bingley felt the same," I laughed.

We walked in comfortable silence for a few moments before Jane spoke again. "Lizzy, may I ask you something?"

"Of course," I said, turning toward her.

"It's about Mr. Darcy," Jane said hesitantly. "And what you told me about what happened at Lady Blackridge's ball—"

I sighed, my gaze falling to the ground. "I don't know, Jane. He apologized and promised to speak to Miss Howe on my behalf—but I do not know what good it will do. Part of me wants to believe him, but the other part of me can't forget what was said about him. And about me— My reputation, such as it was, was forgotten in almost a moment because of— because of what? I fear I do not understand."

"Jealousy," Jane said firmly. "Almost certainly. Miss Howe has obviously been threatened by Mr. Darcy choosing to dance with you—"

"But it is such a petty thing!"

"Is Mr. Darcy worth such a fuss?" Jane asked after a moment.

I let out a heavy sigh, but I could not keep the smile from my lips as I thought of the gentleman. "He is... unlike any other gentleman I've met before."

Jane laughed. "That's because he's a rich, handsome gentleman. They're not exactly a common sight in Hertfordshire."

I laughed, feeling some of the tension leaving my body. "This is very true... but in London one might throw a ha'penny and strike several at once!"

"Then what must it be that could drive a young woman to such lengths to keep you apart?"

"Nonsense," I said with a shake of my head. "Utter nonsense. I do not understand the young ladies in London. Why, Miss Trainor would not even speak to me after the ball!"

"Alas," Jane said, "she was very nice... I was quite surprised to hear that she had behaved in such a manner."

"I cannot blame her," I said. "If my reputation was called into question, then it could stain anyone who kept company with me..."

"It is a very good thing that you do not care what anyone in London thinks," Jane said.

"Indeed."

As we walked, I couldn't help but feel a sense of unease.

There was something about Mr. Darcy that drew me to him, but I couldn't shake the feeling that he was hiding something from me.

But what could it be? *And why did I care so much?*

SIX
darcy

IF CHARLES HAD HOPED that his presence in Hertfordshire would go unnoticed, I would have called him a fool.

Before long, word had spread that Netherfield Park had been let to a wealthy, unmarried, gentleman. Charles had not, of course, signed any papers that would confirm his status as the new occupant of the estate—but I knew that he had already made up his mind, and the rumors that swirled through the small country town just five miles down the road seemed to be enough to secure his sentiments.

The estate was also beset by visitors—polite ones, it must be said. But visitors.

Country gentlemen with little to recommend them in the way of social position or fortune, but each of them with an unmarried daughter or a wife who was eager to elevate the family station just a little with an advantageous marriage.

Sir William Lucas was the only personage of note in Hertfordshire—certainly the only titled member of its society, and while Charles found him endlessly amusing, I found the older man's bluster tedious.

But it was not Sir William that occupied my thoughts as I walked through the gardens of Netherfield Park. It was Elizabeth Bennet.

The Bennet sisters had returned to Netherfield Park several times since our arrival, and each visit was more enjoyable than the last. I was also certain that Charles was halfway in love with the eldest Bennet daughter, if not completely in love with her...

But Elizabeth occupied my thoughts like no woman ever had before. She was quick-witted and independent, with a sharp tongue that cut to the heart of a matter and set my head to spinning, not knowing whether I should laugh at what she had said or if I should take her at her word... Each time I thought I knew the answer, I found that I was completely wrong. It was infuriating and intriguing, and I could never predict what she might say or do next.

I had apologized for Miss Howe's behavior towards her at Lady Blackridge's ball, but I knew that it was not enough to earn her trust. There was a wall between us that I could not seem to break through.

But I was determined to try.

As I walked, lost in thought, I suddenly heard the sound of footsteps behind me. I turned to find Miss Bennet walking towards me, a small smile on her lips.

"Mr. Darcy," she said. "My sister and I were taking a turn about the gardens and I couldn't help but notice you walking alone. Will you join us?"

I nodded and fell into step beside her. "Of course."

As we walked, I found myself at a loss for words. It was not often that I was left speechless, but there was something about Elizabeth that made me feel inadequate in her presence.

"I hope you are enjoying your stay in Hertfordshire," she said at last, breaking the silence.

"I am," I replied with a smile. "It is a beautiful part of the country."

"Yes, it is. It is a shame that our society is so... limited. Will you be attending the assembly? Lady Lucas has already sent out her invitations, and I know that you would not have been missed—"

"No, indeed," I said. "We received the invitation from Sir William's own hand. I believe the ink was still a bit damp."

Elizabeth laughed. "Unsurprising, I must say. Sir William has two daughters in need of a good husband, and I daresay that Lady Lucas will have pushed him out the door as soon as the invitations were written."

"Indeed," I replied. Sir William had seemed somewhat embarrassed in his last visit, perhaps that was the reason. Pressure to deliver.

We continued walking in companionable silence for a few moments before Elizabeth spoke again. "I must apologize, Mr. Darcy."

"For what?" I was truly surprised at her words.

"I have..." She frowned a moment and then glanced at me before she continued. "I confess that I have held some resentment toward you. For what happened at the ball. It was not your fault, of course, but that did not stop me from believing that it might have been. Did you— Did you choose to dance with me because you were interested in... in me. Or was there another reason for it?"

I cleared my throat, unsure of how to proceed without causing her more distress. "I understand," I said, keeping my tone even. "I must admit—and you must forgive me—that I was, indeed inspired to dance with you to avoid another... responsibility."

"I see."

"But— I said that you must forgive me—the more time I spent in your company, the less I wished to leave it."

Her frown deepened, and she did not look at me. I had ruined everything with my honesty, I was certain of that much.

"I was not at my best that evening," I said in a rush.

"No, you were not," she agreed with a small smile. "You are not like the other gentlemen that I have met, Mr. Darcy. You have a depth to you that is rare, and a seriousness that is refreshing. But perhaps I am too used to officers and country gentlemen who do not dream beyond the borders of Hertfordshire."

I felt a smile tug at the corners of my lips. "Thank you, Miss Bennet. That is a compliment indeed."

"It is the truth," she said with a nod. "And I do not say such things lightly."

We reached the end of the garden path, and Elizabeth turned to me with a small smile. "Thank you for keeping me company, Mr. Darcy. I must go and find my sister, but I hope that we can speak again soon."

"I hope so as well," I said, watching as she walked away.

The moment of reverie was broken almost in an instant as I heard the approach of footsteps from around the corner of the house. "Darcy! There you are!" Charles' frantic voice echoed off the stones. His cheeks were ruddy and his eyes were bright with anger.

"What is it, man?" I demanded.

"It is Caroline," he said. "She has written that she is coming to Netherfield Park... and she is bringing Miss Howe with her—at the request of Lady Catherine de Bourgh."

I laid a hand against the sun-warmed stone of the house to steady myself.

"I— What? But your sister loathes the countryside. She tells me so in no uncertain terms every time you visit Pemberley."

"I know," Charles said with a shake of his head. "She is doing it purely to vex me, I know it. She hates the thought of my becoming a country gentleman. I could actually be happy here, Darcy! How dare she—"

"Indeed," I murmured. But I was not concerned with Caroline's designs on foiling her brother's happiness—no, no. Caroline was coming to Hertfordshire with an entirely different mission.

To ruin mine.

* * *

AWAITING Caroline's arrival was like waiting for a storm to sweep over the countryside. One could see it looming in the distance and far too much time was spent wondering what sort of damage it would wreak upon the fields and the gardens that had been so painstakingly tended...

And she was bringing Miss Clarissa Howe with her.

At my aunt's request.

I knew that I should tell Elizabeth—she had been convinced that her reputation would be safe with London far behind her. But Caroline was bringing London to Hertfordshire. And if I knew small town gossips, whatever news that could be had from London would be gobbled up in an instant without a second thought given to its origins.

Especially scandalous news.

With each day that passed, the threat of Caroline's arrival loomed larger in my mind. Charles begged me to wait until the Bennet sisters came to visit, but I agonized over it, worried that Caroline and Clarissa Howe would arrive before I had a chance to warn Elizabeth.

When Jane and Elizabeth did finally pay a visit to Netherfield Park, Charles was more than content to speak to Jane about some of the repairs that he meant to make to the house— repairs which Mr. Jarrett would have to agree to, and which he may eventually have to pay for... something which I was certain that the elderly man would wish to avoid. I had counseled Charles to ask for a lower priced lease on the estate with the promise that he would tend to the repairs himself... but the decision was, ultimately, Mr. Jarrett's. I was invested in the outcome of their conversation, of course, but speaking to Elizabeth took precedence.

"Are you quite well, Mr. Darcy?" she asked at once.

"I am, I thank you," I replied quickly. "But there is something I must speak to you about, most urgently."

Elizabeth's eyebrow rose. "Urgently?"

"Indeed." I gestured toward the corridor and Elizabeth hesitated only a moment as she glanced toward her sister, but Jane and Mr. Bingley were deep in conversation as Charles explained his plans for the house and Jane did not look up from the notes she was making. Elizabeth's lips pressed into a thin line and then she nodded and walked out of the parlor. She stood in the corridor, waiting for me, her hands clasped at her waist.

Guilt weighed heavily on my shoulders.

I should have dealt with Miss Clarissa Howe before I had departed London.

I knew that now.

"Miss Bennet— What happened to you in London, it was... unfortunate."

Elizabeth's smile faded somewhat. "Unfortunate."

"Yes, indeed. But you must know that what Miss Howe said about you, it had nothing to do with you... She did not do it out of any animosity towards yourself—"

"Mr. Darcy, are you entirely certain that you know of what

you speak?" she asked. Her expression was incredulous now, but I couldn't stop myself.

"No, indeed. It had everything to do with me— Miss How is, very clearly, a jealous young woman. My aunt, Lady Catherine de Bourgh, had chosen Miss Howe as my future wife—"

"I beg your pardon?"

"And when she saw us dancing together, she, very naturally, assumed that you had usurped her place—"

"Mr. Darcy," she cried. "*You* are the one who asked *me* to dance!"

"Yes... that is true."

"And from what I gathered from Mr. Bingley, you danced with me to avoid any interaction with Miss Howe. Is that also correct?"

Damn.

"It— is."

Elizabeth glared at me, her fine eyes narrowed in anger. "I was nothing more than a convenient escape," she said. "A means to avoid your responsibilities, and your own better judgment. Is that correct?"

"I—"

It was. She was quite correct and the guilt I had felt earlier pressed down upon me. Elizabeth Bennet had made me feel like a fool—and I did not know how to correct it.

"Was that all you had to say?" she demanded.

"No," I managed to choke out. "Miss Howe— She is coming to Hertfordshire. As a guest of Charles' elder sister, Caroline."

Her eyes widened in shock. "What?"

"She is coming here, to stay at Netherfield Park," I replied. "I— I wished to warn you."

Elizabeth's hands clenched into fists at her sides. "I see," she said.

"Elizabeth— I am... I hope you can forgive me—"

"Actions, Mrs. Darcy," she said simply. "Actions... not words. That is what matters. Good day to you."

She turned on her heel and strode away from me without a backward glance.

SEVEN
elizabeth

ALONE IN MY BEDCHAMBER, I paced the floor in front of my bed and tried to make sense of what was happening.

I had not yet told Jane, she had been far too overjoyed with the news that Mr. Bingley's sister was coming to Hertfordshire... I could not burden her with the knowledge that the young woman who accompanied Caroline Bingley had been the architect of the rumors that would have ruined me if I had stayed in London.

I had no doubt that her words had already done some damage to my aunt's reputation... I could only hope that any hurts Mrs. Gardiner had suffered could be easily mended.

Young ladies were prone to gossip—harmful and harmless alike—but I was certain that my aunt's friends could see through such things... especially something as baseless as the rumors that Miss Howe had begun.

Jane would be eager to be introduced to Miss Caroline Bingley, but I could think of nothing I would like *less* than to be in that woman's company. If Miss Howe was coming as her guest, they must be first friends... and anyone who would be friends with a snake like Miss Howe was surely no better.

I longed to share these opinions with my sister, but it could not be done. I could not ruin Jane's happiness. She and Mr. Bingley had been almost inseparable during the weeks since his arrival, and I could see already that she was in love with him.

My mother expected that there would be an engagement announced within weeks, perhaps even before the first leaves of autumn began to turn... surely, the arrival of his elder sister would seal their intentions in place. An elder sister's opinion was sometimes all that was required to solidify an engagement.

If my mother was to be believed, Caroline Bingley would single-handedly convince her brother to cease in his stalling and an offer of marriage would be made at once.

I did not hold out any such hopes, but I would not dare speak of such things.

Not now.

Not ever.

If Mr. Bingley *were* to propose to Jane, I would be thrilled and overjoyed. But I did not think that the presence of his elder sister in Netherfield Park would guarantee any of that.

As I continued to pace, my thoughts began to shift back to Mr. Darcy. I could not deny the anger that I felt towards him for using me as a means of avoiding Miss Howe, and for his thoughtlessness in not warning me earlier. But just as strong was the sense of longing and attraction that I had felt towards him since our first meeting.

After what he had said to me in the garden, I had been determined to dislike him and forget any fondness I might have had for him... he was proud and arrogant, and he had used me. But four days had passed since Jane and I had been at Netherfield Park, and with each passing day, I found myself drawn to him despite my best efforts to resist.

But I could not let myself be swayed by his charms, nor by the way he made me feel as though I was the only one who understood him... Not when Miss Howe's arrival threatened to bring new rumors and accusations against me. If she was truly convinced that I meant to usurp her position, then what would stop her from spreading the same rumors about me here in Hertfordshire. Rumors that could not touch me in London could leave me scarred here in the country.

I needed to be careful, to keep my guard up around everyone, especially Mr. Darcy.

With a sigh, I finally stopped pacing and sat down at my vanity. I glanced at my reflection in the mirror, I wondered what the future held for me here. Would I ever be able to find happiness, or would I forever be plagued by the whispers and gossip of those around me?

As I sat there lost in thought, I heard a knock at my door. I straightened my posture and called out, "Come in." The door opened and Jane walked into the room.

"Lizzy, you do not keep the door closed very often... is everything all right?"

"It is— yes, I am fine," I replied after a short pause.

Jane's eyebrows lifted slightly, but she did not press for a different answer.

"There is wonderful news from Netherfield Park," she began, "Miss Bingley has arrived with her friend—and we have been invited to tea! Is that not wonderful?"

"It is," I said with what I hoped was an encouraging smile. "Mama must be overjoyed to hear this news?"

"She is," Jane sighed. She sat down upon the edge of her bed and her hands twisted in her lap. "Do you really think that she might be right?" she asked.

"That Mr. Bingley is sure to propose?" I paused and pretended to consider her question very carefully until Jane leaned back to grab one of her pillows and thumped me with it.

"Lizzy!"

I laughed and grabbed the pillow out of her hands. "I do," I laughed. "I do think that he will propose. But I also do not think that he requires his sister's permission to do so. He is a grown man, and the head of his household!"

"He has not yet signed the papers to take over Netherfield Park," Jane said. "What if he changes his mind?"

"Well," I said and threw her pillow back, "perhaps you will be the mistress of a London house instead of a country estate... would that suit you very ill?"

"No, indeed," Jane laughed as she caught the pillow and placed it back upon her bed. "But, Lizzy, you will come to tea with me, will you not?"

"Of course," I replied. "I would not leave you alone with two strange women... Who knows what might be said! London is not Meryton..."

"That is an unassailable truth," Jane laughed.

"You must be on your guard," I said. "These women are not like the ones we know here..."

"Lizzy—"

"They are sly and cunning, and would think nothing of destroying anyone who stood in the way of what they wanted —or what they felt that they deserved..."

Jane's laughter faded in an instant. "Lizzy— is something wrong?"

I leaned back against my chair and let out a heavy sigh. "There is."

"What? You must tell me!"

"I had thought to keep it to myself," I said, "but it seems that I will not be able to avoid it."

Jane laid a reassuring hand upon my shoulder and I turned

in my chair to face her. "You remember that I told you about a young lady in London who told terrible rumors about me—and sought to ruin my reputation?"

Jane nodded. "A horrid thing to do to someone you have never met... I couldn't not imagine such a thing."

"That young woman is coming here. To Netherfield Park. As Caroline Bingley's guest."

Jane's eyes widened. "As her guest? Lizzy!"

I nodded. "Miss Clarissa Howe will be here, even now... and we have been invited to tea."

"Oh, Lizzy— and I was so thrilled— I am so sorry—"

I shook my head. "It does not matter. Perhaps it will do me some good to confront her and explain my position. If she believes that I tried to steal Mr. Darcy away from her, I must set her mind at ease."

Jane's expression softened. "Lizzy... I did have another reason to come here to speak with you."

"Oh?"

"I came to speak of Mr. Darcy."

My heart skipped a beat at the mention of his name. "What of him?"

Jane smiled and took my hand. "I know that you are angry at him. But I also know that you have an affection for him."

I pulled my hand away from hers and stood up. "You are mistaken. I have no such feelings for Mr. Darcy. He has shown himself to be nothing more than an arrogant and thoughtless man."

"But I have seen the way you look at him, Lizzy. And the way he looks at you. if there was nothing between you then Miss Howe would have had no reason to speak of you in such a terrible manner. She is threatened by your connection—if even a stranger can see it—"

I shook my head. "You are mistaken."

Jane laughed. "I most certainly am not. You can deny it all you like, but you are a terrible liar, my dearest."

I couldn't help but feel a flicker of anger at Jane's words, though I knew she spoke with the best of intentions.

"Even if what you say is true, it matters not. Mr. Darcy is not a man I could ever love, nor one who I would wish to be associated with." I paused for a moment, considering my words. "In any case, he has made it quite clear that he does not hold me in any esteem. I am not foolish enough to waste any more of my time on him."

Jane's expression softened, and she gave me a sympathetic look. "I understand, Lizzy. But do not be too quick to close yourself off to the possibility of love. It can come in the most unexpected ways. I only wanted to make sure that you were aware of your feelings before Miss Howe arrived and made things worse. You must be careful, Lizzy. You do not want to give her any more ammunition to use against you."

I sighed heavily and sat back down at my vanity. "I know, Jane. I appreciate your concern. I will be careful."

I knew she was right, but I couldn't shake off the feeling of hurt and anger that Mr. Darcy had caused me. I had never felt so insulted and humiliated in all my life.

"All we can do is stay polite," Jane said. "Surely, she cannot be horrid if you are nothing but welcoming and kind. Perhaps if she knows you better—"

I shook my head. "I do not think that would help in the slightest, but for your sake I shall try."

Jane smiled and patted my hand. "You are a wonderful sister," she said. "Perhaps Mama is correct and this will be the final step that Mr. Bingley needs to make his offer of marriage—"

"Perhaps it is," I replied. "Let us hope so."

* * *

AS MUCH AS I wished to avoid taking tea with Caroline Bingley and Miss Howe, I could do nothing to stop the passage of time, nor could I avoid my mother's scheming.

It did not help matters that I couldn't shake the sense of foreboding about the coming encounter with Miss Howe.

I had always prided myself on my ability to hold my own in any social situation, but this was something entirely different. I had no idea what sort of woman she was, or what her motivations were.

All I knew was that she had already made up her mind about me, and that she would stop at nothing to ruin my reputation.

But I was not one to back down from a challenge. I would face Miss Howe head on, and I would not let her ruin my life for the sake of her own pride.

Jane did her best to keep me distracted by other things as we walked down the road toward Netherfield Park, but as the house appeared over the hill, I tried to steel myself for what was to come. I knew that I was walking into a trap, but I couldn't avoid it now.

The moment we arrived, Caroline and Miss Howe descended upon us with all the grace and poise of a pair of vultures, and I could feel a chill run down my spine.

"Miss Jane Bennet, how delightful to see you," Caroline cooed, but her gaze flickered over to Miss Howe, who was wearing a smug smile. "My brother has told me almost nothing about you, so I am most eager to make your acquaintance."

I disliked Caroline Bingley immediately, but my elder sister was much more capable of hiding her emotions than I was, and she smiled graciously at Caroline.

"Miss Bingley, I am overjoyed to finally meet you. Your

brother has spoken of you often, and I feel that I know you already."

"Has he," Caroline purred. "And Miss Eliza Bennet," she said, her focus turning to me. "We have heard ever so much about *you*... I was so hoping to meet you at Lady Blackridge's ball, but you departed in such a hurry— What a pleasure it is to meet the *infamous* Miss Bennet."

"Infamous?" I said with a smile. "Hardly. I am afraid that you will discover that I am nothing of the sort." I was trying to keep my tone light, but I feared that I would crack into pieces at any moment.

Miss Howe's smile widened. "We shall see," she said. "We have heard all sorts of things about you in London, Miss Bennet. But I am sure that they are all just rumors."

Jane coughed discreetly and Caroline smiled and stepped into the parlor. Miss Howe followed her and I glanced at my sister gratefully. I could feel the tension in the air, and I knew that this was only the beginning of what was to come.

"If you will excuse me for just a moment," Jane said. "I should like to speak to the cook and see how she is managing... Mr. Jarrett did ask me to check on her."

"You are kind to do so," Caroline Bingley said. "Please join us as soon as you are able."

"Of course," Jane said with a smile. She laid a hand on my arm. "I shall not be long."

I nodded and tried to smile back, but my stomach was in knots as Jane walked down the corridor toward the kitchens.

As we sat down for tea, I could feel Miss Howe's eyes on me, analyzing my every move. Caroline continued to make small talk, but it was clear that Miss Howe was the one in control of the situation.

"I must say, Miss Bennet, I am surprised that you dared to show your face here," Miss Howe said suddenly, breaking the tension. "After all, I heard that you had quite the reputation in London. I was under the impression that you would have been too ashamed to show your face in polite society again. Hiding in the country—"

I resisted the urge to flinch at her words. "I am not sure what you are referring to, Miss Howe. I have always conducted myself in a respectable manner. And I only visit London occasionally. Not often enough to come under anyone's scrutiny."

Miss Howe laughed. "Oh, come now, Miss Bennet. Everyone has been talking about your activities in London. I have heard that you keep company with officers, and any gentleman who will speak with you for more than a few moments. And your family's connections—or lack thereof—are hardly a secret."

I felt my cheeks grow warm with embarrassment and anger. "I fail to see how my family's standing has anything to do with my character. And whoever has told you about my... company... is mistaken."

Miss Howe simply smiled, but her eyes were cold. "Of course, Miss Bennet. I am sure that is what you would like us all to believe."

It was then that Caroline intervened, sensing the tension in the air. "Miss Bennet, Miss Howe, I cannot help but think that we are getting off on the wrong foot." she said, her voice sugary sweet.

"You are quite correct, Caroline," Miss Howe said, her smile equally sweet. "What do you make of this estate your brother has chosen?"

Caroline's nose wrinkled as she looked at the faded furnishings and then stirred her tea. "Charles has always had a taste for more... common things," she said.

My spine straightened. She was referring to Jane as much as she was referring to the house.

"Netherfield Park has other charms," I said. "It has a

goodly reputation in Hertfordshire, and there are many ways that the house might be improved without too much effort—"

"Improvements are not always necessary, Miss Bennet," Miss Howe said, her voice dripping with condescension. "Some people are content with mediocrity." She turned to Caroline. "Do you not agree, Caroline?"

Caroline smiled thinly. "I suppose it depends on the person."

I gritted my teeth, trying to keep my anger in check. These two women were unbearable, and I could feel my skin crawling with discomfort.

"If you will excuse me," I said, rising from my chair. "I must see what is keeping Jane..."

I could feel their eyes on me as I left the room, but I did not care. I needed a moment to compose myself before I lost my temper completely.

As I stepped into the corridor, I heard Caroline's voice drift after me. "She really is quite horrid, isn't she? Whatever does Mr. Darcy see in her?"

Miss Howe's laughter made my cheeks burn. "I'm certain it's nothing to do with that... if she flings herself in the direction of any gentleman who pays her any attention—"

I stopped dead in my tracks, my fists clenched.

How dare she? How dare they?

I was not going to let them get the best of me.

I turned back to face them and marched into the room, my eyes blazing. "You may say whatever you like about me behind my back, Miss Bingley," I said, my voice low and controlled. "But I will not tolerate such insults in my presence. And as for you, Miss Howe," I said, stepping closer to her. "I do not know what your motivations are, but I do know that I will not allow you to ruin my reputation for the sake of your own amusement.

I suggest you mind your tongue in the future. You do not even know me."

With that, I turned and walked out of the room, my head held high. I could feel their eyes on my back, but I refused to let them see me falter.

As I walked through the halls of Netherfield, my anger fuelled my steps. I had made a mistake in allowing my emotions to overtake my better sensibilities, but I could not allow them to continue to insult me without some reaction.

I knew that Caroline Bingley and Miss Howe would not take kindly to my words, and I feared what they might do to me in retaliation.

But I refused to let them get the best of me. I was not going to let their cruel words define me.

As I reached the door that led to the kitchens, I paused outside the door, taking a deep breath to steady myself before I pushed open the door.

Jane stood just outside the kitchen, her expression was pained, but she smiled when she saw me.

"Are you alright, Jane?" I asked.

Jane nodded. "Yes, Lizzy, of course. Mrs. Evans is somewhat worse for wear, I do not think she was prepared for the sudden arrival of guests with such... exacting tastes. But I am more worried about you. I saw the way they were looking at you."

I shrugged and did my best to appear nonchalant. "It was nothing, Jane. Just a bit of unpleasantness. But we mustn't let them get the best of us."

Jane smiled, but her eyes were filled with concern. "I know, Lizzy. But please be careful. I don't trust Miss Bingley *or* Miss Howe."

I nodded, my mind racing. Jane was right to be concerned. But I couldn't let my fear stop me. I had to be strong, for both of us.

"Come, we shall return to the parlor. I promised Mr. Bingley that I would be well acquainted with his sister, and I mean to keep that promise. If she is horrid, then I shall have to bear it for his sake."

I let out a long breath and nodded. "Of course, Jane. I will not allow my emotions to overtake me again. But I must take some air before I return to the parlor... will you make my apologies?"

"I will," Jane replied.

My sister embraced me tightly and then left me in the corridor as she returned to the parlor. I took a deep breath and then walked through the kitchen and out the door into the small herb garden and vegetable patch that had been planted so many years ago. Mrs. Evans had done as best she could to keep it tidy and growing well, but she needed help to keep the garden free of weeds and pests... I could see where the rabbits had come in to nibble at the rhubarb and resolved to suggest that Mr. Bingley hire a gardener to help tend the garden beds and the flowers that Mr. Jarrett was so proud of.

How long could I remain in the garden before I was missed?

I could see the windows of the parlor from my position in the garden, and I could see the back of Miss Howe's head and her elegant hairstyle. How I longed to throw a beetroot at her.

The thought of the look on her face made me laugh, and I covered my mouth to keep my mirth to myself.

I must face her again, and hope that my words had been enough to silence her for a little while. I doubted very much that she would feel any shame for what she had said about me, but I would be grateful for any reprieve... If Miss Howe was to be my enemy, I needed time to prepare my defense.

EIGHT
darcy

CHARLES HAD WARNED me that his sister would invite Jane and Elizabeth Bennet to tea, and for once he seemed just as nervous and out of sorts as I felt.

"Do you really think this was a good idea?" Charles blurted out.

The stables were quiet, and the farthest away from the house that we could get. An ideal position, in my opinion.

"Would you have preferred to stay in the house," I asked over the back of my gelding.

Charles made a face. "Indeed not," he said. "But that is not what I meant. I meant—do you think it was a good idea to allow Caroline to invite the Bennet sisters for tea?"

"Ah. Of course not," I replied. "But if you wish to have Caroline's approval of your choice of wife—"

"I do not need it," Charles huffed.

"Of course you do not," I said. "But, she is here... and they are having tea. Will Caroline's opinion change your impression of Miss Jane Bennet in the slightest?"

"Would Georgiana's change your opinion of Miss Elizabeth Bennet?"

I glared at my friend, but his grin was teasing. "I would hope that she and Georgiana would be good friends," I said after a moment. "But, no. I would not choose someone who would dislike my sister."

"You are fortunate that Georgiana is such a sweet girl," Charles said. "Caroline is very full of... opinions."

A judicious observation.

I chuckled and stroked the brush over my gelding's flank.

"And what of Miss Howe," Charles said. "You have not spoken to her since she arrived. Caroline tells me that the young lady is very vexed by your avoidance of her."

"I am certain of it," I said through gritted teeth.

"What are you going to do about it?" Charles pressed.

"What is there to do?"

Charles leaned on his horse's rump and stared at me. "Are you really going to allow Lady Catherine de Bourgh to pressure you into a marriage you do not want?"

"Of course not," I spluttered.

But Charles was right. That was what I was allowing to happen. By my inactions I was being steadily forced down a path I did not wish to take.

But what *did* I want?

My aunt wished for me to choose a wife—but why did I have to choose one of her design?

Suddenly, an idea came to me.

"You are quite correct, Charles. I need to face Miss Howe and tell her the truth."

Charles' eyebrow rose. "And what truth is that?"

"That while I wish to be married. I do not wish to be married to *her*."

Charles made a face. "Oh, that sounds... dangerous."

"Do not worry, Charles. I have it all well in hand."

"I do not like the sound of that," Charles said. "Will you not tell me your plan?"

I shook my head and returned to brushing my horse. The gelding whickered and shifted on his feet. He was eager for a ride, and I was eager to indulge him. But not yet.

First I would have to deal with Miss Howe. I could not allow her to terrorize Miss Bennet any longer. She was behaving as though Lady Catherine's unearned endorsement had made her untouchable and I could not allow that falsehood to continue.

* * *

I WAITED in the corridor as the others settled themselves into the drawing room. Dinner had been excruciating, but I had managed to get through it without too much trouble. The conversation was light, and mostly centered around Caroline distaste for the countryside, and her complaints about the house.

"Charles you must tell that Evans woman that her roast is terrible," Caroline exclaimed. "Overcooked *again*. How does one manage such a thing two nights in a row?"

"Country cooking," Miss Howe said with a small smile. "Surely these people have toughened their stomachs and their palettes to tolerate such things."

"Charles you *cannot* sign those papers," Caroline complained. "This house is an embarrassment. Think of what Louisa would say—and all of our friends in London! No one would come to visit us!"

I entered the drawing room at that moment, and Caroline's eyes lit up with a dangerous glimmer as she saw me. "Ah, Mr. Darcy," she said smoothly. "How delightful of you to join us. Do come in and join us. Charles is on his third glass of whiskey and I fear he might be ill."

I could feel Miss Howe's eyes on me, but I ignored her for the moment as I made my way to the sideboard to pour myself a glass of the same whiskey that Charles favored. My friend was facing the window and he did not turn to defend himself or say anything against his sister's observation.

"How was your tea this afternoon?"

Caroline let out an agonized groan and held out her empty claret glass to be refilled. I set down my whiskey and picked up the decanter of claret.

Instead of filling her glass, I set it down on the table in front of Caroline and returned to the sideboard to retrieve my own drink.

Caroline's face twisted in anger, but before she could say anything, Miss Howe spoke up.

"It was a most tedious teatime, wouldn't you agree, Caroline? These country girls and their country manners—it is a wonder that they are welcome in polite society at all. I shudder to think of what kind of society *is* considered polite so far from London!"

Caroline laughed. "Miss Howe has hit upon the heart of it, has she not, Charles?"

"I do wonder if the ladies of Hertfordshire know the truth about the young ladies they allow in the company of their daughters," Miss Howe said. "I know I would be plagued by guilt if I did not share what I know about Miss Elizabeth Bennet—"

I must have made a noise, for Miss Howe glanced at me in surprise. "What is it, Mr. Darcy?"

"Miss Howe, have you ever met Lady Catherine de Bourgh?"

Miss Howe looked taken aback, but quickly composed herself. "I have not had the honor, Mr. Darcy," she said. "But my mama has come very close—you know that we were quite honored and surprised by her letters... They were quite complimentary. But I'm certain that you are aware of that fact."

"Indeed," I said.

"Mr. Darcy," Caroline interjected. "Might I ask why you have been avoiding Miss Howe? I did not wish to mention anything, but it seemed like the appropriate time."

Did it now.

I hesitated for a moment before deciding to be truthful. "Indeed," I said and then turned to the young lady. "I had intended to say this to you in a more private setting, but Caroline is intent on making this a public affair." I took a breath and ignored the bright pink of Miss Howe's cheeks. "Miss Howe, I have been avoiding you because I do not wish for there to be any misunderstanding between us. I am not interested in pursuing a relationship with you beyond whatever friendly acquaintance there might be."

Miss Howe's eyes widened in shock, but she quickly regained her composure. "I see," she said coolly. "And how will your aunt react to such an... announcement?"

"She will respect my wishes, of course," I said.

"Will she," Caroline countered. "I daresay she will be expecting that there should be some explanation for this... rejection of such a worthy young lady. A case of nerves will not be enough for her, Mr. Darcy, surely you know that as well as I do!"

Charles chuckled, but did not turn around.

"Come now, Mr. Darcy," Caroline pressed. "What could possibly be the reason?" She paused for just a moment and then leaned forward and set her wine glass down upon the table. She lifted the decanter of claret and swirled the dark liquid slowly while she looked at me. "Surely, you are not already engaged?"

Was that the only way to halt this conversation? Was this the only way I would be able to be rid of this nonsense?

"I am," I said briskly.

"To whom?" Miss Howe cried. "If it is that horrid—"

"It is Miss Elizabeth Bennet," I blurted out.

There was silence in the room and I could feel all eyes upon me as I took a sip of my whiskey. I had said it now, and there was no taking it back.

"It cannot be," Miss Howe gasped. "I— I— I do not know what to say."

"I do apologize, Miss Howe, that you came to Netherfield Park under the impression that you would leave here with an engagement," I said.

Caroline scoffed. "Mr. Darcy, I cannot believe that you would throw away your reputation and your family's reputation for the sake of a country girl. You do realize that your aunt will be scandalized?"

"I am well aware of the consequences of my actions, Caroline," I replied evenly. "But Elizabeth Bennet is not just any country girl. She is intelligent, witty, and has a kindness and strength of character that far surpasses any other young lady I have met."

"You are deluding yourself, Mr. Darcy," Miss Howe said, her voice hardening. "Elizabeth Bennet is nothing but a silly, impertinent girl with no connections or prospects. You are making a grave mistake."

I stood up from my chair, the anger I had been trying to keep at bay finally boiling over. "Enough," I said, my voice tight with fury. "I will not stand for your insults. If you cannot respect my choice, then I suggest you leave now."

Caroline stood up abruptly, her face contorted with anger. "This cannot be happening," she spat. "Charles, you must do something!"

Charles finally turned around and looked at his sister. His expression was unreadable, but I could see a sparkle of mischief in his eyes. It was not often that he was able to see his sister in such a state. "There is nothing to be done, Caroline. William has made his choice, and we must respect that."

"But he cannot marry that country nobody!" Caroline exclaimed. "What will everyone think?"

Miss Howe stood up slowly, her face twisted with fury. "You will regret this decision."

Caroline's face was red with indignation, but before she could say anything more her brother stepped forward and laid a firm hand upon her shoulder. "That's *enough*, Caroline," he said. "You've been nothing but a thorn in everyone's side since you arrived here. I suggest you ladies both retire to your rooms and get some rest."

Caroline opened her mouth to protest, but thought better of it and swept out of the room with Miss Howe following closely behind her.

Charles turned to me with a smile. "Well done, old chap," he said, clapping me on the back. "I never thought I'd see the day when Caroline would be speechless."

I shook my head and tried not to laugh.

"Is this really what you planned to do?"

"No, indeed not," I replied.

"Is it true?"

"No. Indeed not."

Charles let out a low whistle. "And what are you going to do about this? Caroline will— You do not need me to tell you that this is not a good idea. Does Miss Bennet know of your plans?"

"No," I hissed. "She does not."

Charles shook his head and took a sip of his whiskey. "I do not envy you, William," he said. "This will not be easy."

"No, it will not."

I had to speak to Elizabeth Bennet... as soon as possible.

NINE
elizabeth

I HAD STILL NOT GOTTEN over our teatime at Netherfield Park. Caroline Bingley was dangerous, and Miss Clarissa Howe—it did not matter what I said, she had managed to bring the conversation back to my failings or a sharp comment about my appearance, the shabbiness of Netherfield Park, or our life in the countryside.

Jane had performed marvelously, of course, and if Caroline Bingley was immune to my sister's charms, then I would judge her most harshly.

Although, I did not expect that Caroline Bingley would ever approve of Jane as a match for her younger brother.

I should speak to Charles Bingley to be certain that he would not take anything she might say to heart—nor, indeed, anything that Miss Clarissa Howe might say about *me*.

Jane agonized over the tea as much as I did—but I knew that her worry was entirely focused on Caroline Bingley's acceptance of her.

"Do you think we shall be invited back?" she asked one morning as we sat in the parlor.

Only two days had passed, and our mother asked every day,

several times a day, if another invitation had come from Netherfield Park.

"I cannot say," I replied without looking up from my book. I did not wish for Jane to see how worried I was. Or how angry I was with Miss Howe, and myself for allowing my emotions to get the best of me. She did not deserve the satisfaction of knowing how angry I actually was.

There was a knock at the front door, and Jane and I both looked up in surprise. Kitty and Lydia raced down the corridor to answer the door, shouting and jostling against each other as they went. I gritted my teeth and hoped that it was not anyone of consequence.

"Are you expecting anyone," Jane asked.

I closed my book. "No, certainly not. Perhaps it is Charlotte — The Meryton assembly is only a few days away. She may need our help—"

"Lizzy," Lydia screeched from the foyer. "Come at once!"

Jane's eyes were wide as I set aside my book and stood. I smoothed down my skirts and brushed my curls away from my face as I walked to the door and down the corridor. Kitty and Lydia's bright laughter echoed from the foyer and my stomach tightened. It was not Charlotte—they never stayed to talk to Charlotte.

And then I heard a gentleman's voice. One I recognized.

Mr. Fitzwilliam Darcy.

"Girls," I snapped. "I think you should go to the kitchens and see if Mrs. Hill needs any help with supper."

Kitty and Lydia giggled and tugged on each other's arms before they finally retreated down the corridor.

"He's very handsome, Lizzy," Kitty shouted as they shrieked with laughter and ran toward the kitchen. My cheeks burned, but there was no hiding it.

I forced myself to smile at the gentleman who stood in the doorway.

"Mr. Darcy," I said. "You are very welcome to Longbourn, you must forgive my sisters... they are..."

"You do not need to explain," he said with a smile. "Miss Bennet—may I speak with you?"

"Of course," I said. "Will you come in? Jane is in the parlor—"

He shook his head. "I must speak to you in private."

"In... private..." I paused and then pointed to the garden gate. "I shall meet you in the garden," I said. "I shall be there in a moment."

He nodded and walked toward the gate as I closed the door and rushed back to the parlor.

"Lizzy—" Jane said as I entered. "Why is Mr. Darcy in the garden?"

"He came to speak to me," I hissed. "Please... do not tell Mama."

Jane smiled and then nodded. "Of course. I shall keep watch."

I rushed back to the foyer and flung my shawl around my shoulders before I slipped out the front door and rushed toward the garden gate.

"Mr. Darcy," I said as I approached him. "I cannot stay long—"

"Miss Bennet... Elizabeth..."

Hearing my name on his lips sent a thrill down my spine but I struggled to push that feeling down.

"I have something to tell you—something— Something I wish I did not have to tell you."

The smile faded from my lips. "I don't understand—"

"Miss Howe— She intended to do your reputation harm here in Hertfordshire, and I— I could not allow that to happen."

Fear shuddered through me. "She— she told you this?"

He nodded. "Very clearly. But I have done everything in my power to protect you from this. But I need you to understand—"

"Protect me?" I said, bewildered. "How could you do that?"

"By—" He paused and took a breath. He clutched his hat with a white-knuckled grip and my throat tightened. "Miss Bennet, in order to ensure that whatever Miss Howe might have planned to say about you would not affect you, or your family, in any way— I told her that we were engaged."

I stared at him in disbelief.

"You... We are... what?"

"It was the only way," he protested.

My head was spinning.

Engaged? To Mr. Darcy?

The thought had never even crossed my mind. And yet, here he was, standing before me, admitting to lying to protect me from Miss Howe's viciousness.

"But why... why go to such lengths?" I asked, still trying to process the situation.

"I could not bear the thought of your reputation being tarnished," he explained, his voice low and intense.

I shook my head, trying to make sense of what he was saying. "But we are *not* engaged, Mr. Darcy. Why would you say such a thing?"

"I understand that this is sudden and perhaps not what you might have wished—" he began, but I interrupted him.

"I *never* wished for this, Mr. Darcy. I never wished for any engagement at *all*. And *certainly* not to you!" I said, my voice rising in anger.

"I am aware of that," he said calmly. "But it was necessary at the time. And now, I must ask for your help in keeping up this facade, at least for a little while longer."

"Why must we keep it up at all?" I protested, my eyes narrowing in suspicion. "What is it that you want from me, Mr. Darcy?"

"I want nothing from you, Miss Bennet," he said firmly. "I merely wish to protect your reputation and that of your family. It was a difficult decision to make, but I felt that it was necessary."

"And did you think about how this might affect *me*?" I asked, my voice trembling with emotion. "Did you think about what it would mean for me to be engaged to a man like you?"

His face darkened, and for a moment, I thought he would be angry with me. But then, he took a deep breath and spoke in a quiet voice. "I understand that this is not what you would have wanted, Miss Bennet. But please, you must understand that I did not do this lightly. And if there was any other way, I would have taken it."

"But— you do not understand," I protested. "What will happen when Miss Howe returns to London? Will you break our engagement and leave me here to face the consequences of that?"

Darcy frowned and looked away. He had, very clearly, not thought about the repercussions of his hasty decision.

"I—"

"I shall think on it," I snapped. "In the meantime, you will say nothing further of this to anyone. If Miss Howe is the only one who knows—"

"Caroline Bingley was also in the room... and Mr. Bingley."

I gritted my teeth to keep from crying out in anger.

"I see," I hissed.

"Caroline has received Lady Lucas' invitation to the Meryton assembly," he continued.

"And you would like to attend as a couple so that everyone might see us together," I said.

He nodded. "You have it correct."

I straightened my shoulders and met his dark gaze boldly. "Well, then you must stay and speak to my father, otherwise this will come as a terrible shock to him, and my mother. I do not envy you this discussion, but I hope that you will be honest with him. My father does not like liars."

The gentleman nodded, his expression serious. "I understand. I will speak to your father at once, and I will tell him the truth."

"And what will you say to him?" I asked, my eyes fixed on his.

"I will tell him that I lied about our engagement to protect your reputation," he replied, his voice firm.

I nodded and felt a sense of relief wash over me. At least he was willing to come clean to my father.

"Very well," I said as I turned away from him. "I suppose I shall see you at the Meryton assembly."

"Elizabeth," he said softly. He reached out to touch my arm. "Please understand that I did what I thought was best."

"I understand, Mr. Darcy," I said as I pulled away from him. "But that does not mean I have to like it."

With that, I turned and walked back toward the house and left him standing alone in the garden. A mixture of emotions rushed through me—anger, confusion, betrayal, and even a hint of attraction.

Despite my misgivings about Mr. Darcy, there was still something about him that drew me in, something that made me want to know him better. He had done this to protect me. A rash decision to be sure, but for now, I had to focus on the task at hand—keeping up the facade of this engagement, at least until we could figure out a way to undo the damage that had been done.

"Come along, Mr. Darcy," I called out. "I shall take you to my father."

The gentleman let out a surprised grunt and hurried to follow me back to the house.

My father would have stern words for him, that much I could be certain of. I should have felt some pity for him, but I could not find it in me.

* * *

MY MOTHER'S joyful screeching filled the house. Unlike her other outbursts, I could not hide from this one...

"My own Lizzy, engaged to a gentleman as fine as Mr. Fitzwilliam Darcy— Did you know, Jane? He has a *grand* estate in Derbyshire. And we shall *all* visit for Christmastide!"

Jane nudged me with her elbow. "Lizzy, are you all right?"

I nodded. Jane knew everything now. But I did not know how I was supposed to bear all of this. The Meryton assembly would be... agonizing.

"Now, Lizzy," my mother's voice echoed in the corridor as she approached the parlor. "You will wear the gown you brought home from London—it is far too fine for an assembly, but you must be the best dressed young lady in attendance! I will not accept any arguments!"

"Of course, Mama," I murmured.

Miss Trainor's lilac gown, the one she had refused to take back after Lady Blackridge's ball, lay in its box in my wardrobe. I had not even had the heart to look at it. It was the gown I had been wearing when all of this began...

AS THE EVENING of the Meryton assembly approached, my nerves were stretched thin. The thought of being seen in public with Mr. Darcy, pretending to be engaged, filled me with a sense of dread. Nevertheless, I knew it was necessary to protect my family's reputation.

Jane had done her best to try to calm my nerves—I could admit that I enjoyed Mr. Darcy's company and that we had much in common despite the difference in our social standing... He loved the same books and we had similar opinions on many things... But this— I did not know if I could forgive this. I was still reeling from his admission that he had only danced with me to avoid Miss Howe...

But was my own pride blinding me to what could be?

Jane certainly seemed to think so.

On the night of the assembly, I donned the gown my mother had insisted upon. The color brought out the green in my eyes, but otherwise, I felt uncomfortable in it, but I could not be certain if it was the memories I attached to it or something else.

Mr. Darcy's carriage arrived at Longbourn just as we were preparing to leave, and my father greeted him with a stern nod. I could tell that the gentleman was nervous, but he stood tall and composed.

Lydia and Kitty giggled together as they looked out the window at the carriage and complained about how jealous they were that they were not allowed to accompany us.

"Can we not ride with Lizzy, Mama," Lydia moaned.

"No, you shall not," my mother snapped. "You should be proud and grateful that your elder sister will be arriving in a separate carriage.

"Perhaps, with any luck, Jane will be next!"

My cheeks were hot with embarrassment, but there was nothing I could say.

"Shall we be off then?" Mr. Darcy asked in a low voice, and I nodded, grateful for the cool evening air on my cheeks and the opportunity to escape the embarrassment of the parlor and my mother's effusive fussing.

The carriage ride to the assembly was silent, the only sound was the creak of the wheels and the horses' hooves on the road. I sat opposite Mr. Darcy, my hands clenched in my lap. The tension between us was palpable, and I wondered how long we could keep up this charade.

There was a good deal that I wished to say to him, and none of it was kind. The assembly was the only public event that we would need to attend as a couple—and then... and then I did not know what would happen. My father had told me nothing of his meeting with the gentleman, and Mr. Darcy had not been forthcoming with his plans.

"Try to enjoy yourself," Jane had whispered before we departed.

Her words repeated in my mind, as well as the reminders she had made about the affinity I had with the gentleman. He had done this to save my reputation after all—and that of our entire family.

The carriage turned into the courtyard of the assembly rooms and Mr. Darcy took a deep breath.

"Elizabeth—"

"Do not apologize again," I said.

"But I must," he replied. "I acted rashly and selfishly, and I am sorry for the pain that I caused you."

I hesitated before responding, allowing his words to sink in. His contrition was genuine, and I could not help but feel a twinge of compassion toward him.

"Thank you, Mr. Darcy," I said finally. "I appreciate your apology."

He bowed his head in acknowledgement, and we stepped out of the carriage and made our way into the assembly rooms.

The ballroom was already crowded with people, the sound

of music and conversation filling the air. We were immediately met with curious stares and whispers, and I felt my cheeks heat up with embarrassment as we made our way to a secluded corner of the room.

My mother's shrill voice seemed to overpower even the musicians. She had already begun to gossip with her friends about our engagement. There would be no way to avoid all of the congratulations and well wishes...

I felt a flush of embarrassment as we made our way through the crowd, but Mr. Darcy's strong hand on my arm gave me some comfort.

"Shall we dance?" Mr. Darcy asked as he extended his hand to me.

I hesitated for only a moment before accepting, still uncertain about the situation we found ourselves in. But as we moved onto the dance floor and began to go through the steps of the dance, I felt something... unexpected. It was a feeling that I could not quite place, but it was not entirely unpleasant, either.

As the dance continued, Mr. Darcy and I fell into a comfortable rhythm, our movements complementing each other effortlessly. His hand was warm and steady in mine, and for a moment, I allowed myself to forget about the reasons for our pretend engagement and simply enjoy the moment.

"This is not so terrible," Mr. Darcy said.

I could not be certain if he was speaking to me, or to himself... but he was right. It was not so terrible.

But as we turned about the room, I caught the angry stares of Miss Clarissa Howe and Miss Caroline Bingley and all of the unease I had pushed away rushed to the surface once more.

TEN

darcy

I COULD SEE the change in Elizabeth's expression, and I knew at once that Charles, Caroline and Miss Howe had arrived at the assembly rooms. I had hoped that Elizabeth and I would be able to enjoy at least once more dance—perhaps she might even forget how angry she was with me...

But that was not to be.

"You must forgive me," I began.

"No more apologies," Elizabeth said shortly. "We are here to enjoy ourselves as a couple who has just newly declared our love for each other."

I stared at her in surprise.

"Are we not?" she hissed.

"Yes, of course," I replied quickly.

"Good," she said and then she smiled as we continued to progress through the steps of the dance. It was easy to be with her. Easy to be myself...

Why had I not seen it sooner?

Why had I found myself in two impossible situations when I should have just followed my instincts—which always led me to her.

"How angry does Caroline Bingley look?" Elizabeth whispered.

I glanced at Charles' sister. Her elegant face was red with fury, a most unbecoming shade. "Extremely."

"And Miss Howe?"

"Uncomfortable."

Elizabeth smiled. "Good."

"You will be happy to know that Mr. Bingley and Jane are also upon the dance floor," I said.

"That is wonderful to hear," Elizabeth murmured. "Do you think he will give any weight to his sister's opinion of Jane?"

"Certainly not," I chuckled.

Elizabeth's hand tightened on mine and I tried not to smile.

Perhaps she did have some affection for me.

But as the dance came to an end, Elizabeth quickly dropped my hand and curtsied before me. "Thank you for the dance, Mr. Darcy," she said before turning and making her way to her sisters.

I watched her retreating form, the warmth of her hand still lingering in mine. I knew I had to tell her the truth soon, that our engagement was a ruse to protect her reputation and nothing more. But how could I let her go after experiencing these moments of true connection?

I turned as Miss Howe and Caroline Bingley made their way toward me. "Well, Mr. Darcy," she said. "You and Miss Bennet do make a fine couple upon the dance floor, do they not, Clarissa?"

"Indeed," Miss Howe sneered. "But where has your betrothed disappeared to?"

I bristled at her words, but before I could respond, Elizabeth stepped forward. "I am here, Miss Howe," she said with a cool smile. "But perhaps you would prefer to dance with Mr. Darcy instead?"

There was a flash of something in Miss Howe's eyes, but she quickly masked it with a tight smile. "No, thank you. I know better than to get involved with gentlemen who are spoken for," she replied before turning on her heel and walking away.

Caroline's smile was sly as she turned away. "Thank you for coming tonight, Miss Bingley," Elizabeth said. "I am glad you were able to share in the joy of the evening."

"Yes, it's been quite delightful for a country dance," she replied stiffly.

Elizabeth laid her hand upon my arm and smiled up at me. I could not deny that I wished to be the only one she would ever look at in that manner...

It was an unbidden thought, but it lingered on my mind for longer than it should have.

What if she did not wish to end the engagement when Miss Howe and Miss Bingley returned to London?

Perhaps—perhaps there was something more in her touch on my arm, something more in her eyes when she looked at me.

"Should we return to the dance," Elizabeth asked.

"I can think of nothing I would rather do," I replied. We turned without offering Caroline another look, or another word and I relished the thought of the expression on Caroline's face.

Pinched and angry.

Entirely unbecoming of a woman of her social standing.

Delightful.

As we joined the other dancers, Elizabeth's hand was warm in mine and I smiled down at her. "Elizabeth—"

"Yes, William?"

"What— What will you do after—"

She frowned briefly. "When our engagement is done?"

I did not reply.

"I suppose— Well, I am not certain... For women, it is different, I suppose. Breaking an engagement is... difficult."

"What if it did not end?" I blurted out.

Elizabeth did not answer and we continued to dance, neither one of us acknowledging the silence between us. Elizabeth's smile was gracious as she nodded to the other dancers and friends she saw on the edge of the dance floor.

Finally, she looked up at me. The lilac of her gown brought out the green in her hazel eyes, and her beauty took my breath away each time she looked at me. "What do you mean," she whispered.

"I meant precisely what I said."

"That you would wish—"

I nodded.

Her lips pursed and then she laughed and shook her head.

"Elizabeth— Please. I must beg your forgiveness once more... I should have. I should have acknowledged that which was plain from the beginning. I— I have been drawn to you, unavoidably, since the moment we first met."

"And what of the way you have used me, not once, but twice, to avoid the responsibilities that have been placed upon you?"

That stung just a little.

"Could I not make up for it... if given time?"

"Time," Elizabeth snorted and then looked up at me in alarm. I tried my best not to laugh and she glared at me.

"Think about it," I said. "We need not break this engagement, and you would be free to do as you pleased—"

"As Mrs. Darcy..."

"A small side-effect," I said. "I would ask nothing of you—"

"Except to pretend that I was happily married to a wealthy gentleman with an estate in Derbyshire and ten thousand pounds a year?"

I laughed and shook my head in disbelief. "Would that be so difficult?"

"And what if agreeing to this... arrangement kept me from meeting the gentleman who would be the greatest love of my life?" she asked.

I could not not decide if she was teasing me or if she was being serious. Her expression was unreadable and I was at a loss for words.

"I—"

"I shall think on it," she said briskly.

I could hardly believe what I had just proposed. Was I truly willing to continue this charade just to keep Elizabeth by my side? It seemed foolish and selfish, but my heart could not let go of the idea.

When the dance ended, Elizabeth left me and joined her sisters once more. I watched her go, feeling conflicted. Charles and Jane continued to dance, and I had no doubt that he would finally break through his nervousness and hesitation to propose...

But Elizabeth was all I could see. Laughing with her sisters, gossiping with another young woman near the punch table.

On one hand, I knew what I was asking was unfair to her. I was asking her to continue a charade that had been forced upon her, all in the name of protecting her reputation. On the other, I could not deny that the thought of letting her go was unbearable.

The night wore on, and Elizabeth and I danced together several more times. The more time I spent with her, the more I realized how much I wanted her in my life. It was not just about protecting her reputation anymore. I had fallen for her, completely and utterly.

The doubts consumed me, and I found myself withdrawing from the festivities to seek solitude outside in the gardens that surrounded the assembly rooms.

The night air was cool and refreshing, and I paced the

length of the gravel path, as I tried to calm my racing thoughts. And then, in the darkness, I heard footsteps approaching.

"William?" Elizabeth's voice called out, and I turned to see her approaching me. "Are you alright?"

"Yes," I replied, trying to keep my voice steady. "Just needed some fresh air."

She studied me for a moment, and then took a step closer. "You know," she said softly. "I have been thinking about your proposal."

My heart stopped. Had she made a decision already?

"And while it is a tempting offer," she continued. "I cannot help but wonder if it is the right decision for either of us."

I breathed a sigh of relief, grateful that she was at least considering my request. "I understand," I said. "It was a foolish idea, I know."

Elizabeth shook her head. "No, it wasn't foolish," she said and my heart lurched in my chest as she smiled at me. "It was... unexpected. I had thought that you would be eager to end our arrangement at the soonest possible moment."

"I— I confess that I do not."

Elizabeth's smile grew wider, and she stepped even closer to me. Her hand reached out and brushed against my cheek, sending shivers down my spine. "I must admit, William, that I find the prospect of continuing our engagement quite... exciting."

My heart raced as I looked into her eyes. Was she really saying what I thought she was saying?

"I do not wish to be a burden to you, Elizabeth," I said, my voice barely above a whisper.

"I am not a burden," she said fiercely. "I am a partner. And I want to be with you, William. I want to explore this... arrangement, as you call it, and see where it takes us."

I could hardly believe what I was hearing. Elizabeth, the

woman who had been so skeptical of me, who had criticized and challenged me at every turn, was now offering to continue our engagement—for the sheer thrill of it.

I took her hand in mine and leaned in close to her. "Then let us explore it together," I said.

She rose up on her toes and her lips pressed against mine. As we kissed, the world around us faded away. All I could feel was Elizabeth's body pressed up against mine, her warmth and her passion fueled my own. For that moment, nothing else mattered.

But as the kiss broke, reality came crashing back in.

The arrangement we were discussing was not just a game. It was a serious commitment, one that could have consequences for both of us.

"Elizabeth," I said, pulling away from her. "Are you sure about this?"

She looked up at me with a determined expression on her face. "I am sure," she said.

I took a deep breath and nodded. "Then let us continue our engagement," I said, feeling a weight lifted off my shoulders.

She laid her hand in mine and I pulled it to my lips to press a kiss to her knuckles. As we turned back toward the light of the assembly rooms, a cheer and thunderous applause echoed in the night air.

"What could have happened?" Elizabeth asked.

"I believe Charles has finally made his decision... and it seems that your sister is in agreement."

Elizabeth gasped and tugged on my hand, pulling me back toward the entrance to the hall.

As we made our way back inside the assembly rooms, I felt a sense of excitement and trepidation. We were embarking on a risky and unconventional path, but it felt right.

For the first time in a long time, I felt like I was truly alive.

And with Elizabeth at my side there was nothing I could not face. A convenient escape had led me to the greatest adventure of my life... and I could not ask for a better partner in it.

THE END

Ingram Content Group UK Ltd.
Milton Keynes UK
UKHW020721260623
424053UK00014B/654